The Enchanted Bellows

and

Other Stories

by

ENID BLYTON

Illustrated by
Dorothy Hamilton

AWARD PUBLICATIONS LIMITED

For further information on Enid Blyton please visit
www.blyton.com

Text copyright is the property of Enid Blyton Limited
(a Chorion company). All rights reserved.

ISBN 978-1-84135-447-7

Text copyright © Enid Blyton Limited
Illustrations copyright © 1996 Award Publications Limited

Enid Blyton's signature is a trademark of Enid Blyton Limited

This edition entitled *The Enchanted Bellows and Other Stories*
published by permission of Enid Blyton Limited

First published by Award Publications Limited 1996
This edition first published 2005
Second impression 2008

Published by Award Publications Limited,
The Old Riding School, The Welbeck Estate,
Worksop, Nottinghamshire, S80 3LR

Printed in Singapore

CONTENTS

The
Enchanted Bellows

Once upon a time there were two little imps called Bubble and Squeak. They lived in Puff Cottage, and they made bellows. They sold them for a penny each, and made quite a lot of money. They carved animals on the handles, and all the fairies came to buy them because they were so well-made and pretty.

Now Bubble was good and Squeak was naughty. Squeak was always trying to make Bubble do things he shouldn't, but usually Bubble wouldn't do them. Then one day Squeak had a very strange idea.

"Bubble!" he said, in an excited whisper. "Let's get a wind-spell from the Blowaway Witch, and put it into a pair of bellows! Then we'll sell them to someone we don't like, and see what happens!"

"Don't be naughty," said Bubble. "And stop whispering in my ear like that. It tickles."

"But Bubble, oh Bubble, do let's!" said Squeak. "It's the loveliest idea I've ever had. Just think how funny it would be to put a spell into a pair of bellows! Why, they'd blow and blow and blow all by themselves, and it would be such a joke."

Squeak began to laugh, and when he laughed Bubble simply had to do the same, because Squeak's laugh went on and on like a bubbling stream. And as soon as Bubble began to laugh he felt just as naughty as Squeak.

"All right," he said, when he had got his breath again. "Let's go to the Blowaway Witch now, before I change my mind."

So off they went. The Blowaway Witch lived on the top of a steep hill, and was friends with the South Wind. There was always a breeze round her cottage, and her chimney smoke never went straight up into the sky. It was always blown this way and that.

The two imps were very much out of

6

breath when they at last reached the cottage. They knocked at the door, and the witch came to open it.

"What do you want?" she said.

"Please could you let us have a wind-spell?" asked Squeak.

"What for?" asked the witch.

"To put into one of our pairs of bellows," said Bubble, going red.

"But that would be naughty," said the witch. "Besides, the spell is fivepence, and I am sure you haven't got so much money as that."

7

"Yes, we have," said Squeak, and he took out a bright new fivepence. "Please let us have the spell, dear witch."

Just at that moment the South Wind came to the door too, for he happened to be having tea with the Blowaway Witch, and had heard all that the imps had said.

"Give them the spell," he said. "They can't do any harm with it!"

So the witch took down her box of spells, and looked inside for a wind-spell. She took out one that was not very strong, but just as she was going to hand it to Bubble, she dropped it. The South Wind picked it up, but before he gave it to the imps he breathed on it.

"That will make it ten times as strong as the strongest wind-spell that ever was made!" he thought to himself in glee, for he was a very mischievous fellow. "They will get more than they bargain for! What fun!"

The two imps knew nothing of this. They took the spell, said thank you, paid the witch, and went off down the hill. When they got home they made a fine pair of bellows with ducks carved on the handle, and then with much laughter they pushed the wind-spell right into the very middle of the bellows.

"Now as soon as anyone uses these, the wind-spell will start working, and blow everything all about the room!" chuckled Bubble and Squeak. "Ooh, wouldn't we like to see it!"

They wondered who would buy the bellows, and they decided to wait until someone they didn't like at all came along. And that someone arrived the very next day.

It was Grunts, the old gnome from the bluebell wood. He was very bad-tempered and rude, and the imps disliked him very much. So they thought they would sell him the enchanted bellows.

"My bellows are broken," said Grunts. "I want a new pair. Show me some."

So the imps showed him a lot, and then they took out the enchanted pair. The ducks on the handle were beautifully carved, and Grunts liked them.

"How much are these?" he asked.

"Only a halfpenny," said Squeak. "The others are all a penny each."

"Then I'll take the halfpenny pair," said Grunts, and he put a bent and battered halfpenny down on the counter. Bubble wrapped the bellows up in brown paper, and gave them to the gnome.

Off he went, and the two imps looked at one another and laughed.

"Let's follow him and see what happens!" said Bubble, feeling very naughty indeed.

So they followed Grunts to his home in the bluebell wood. He lived not far away from the palace of the Fairy King and Queen, and had a very nice little cottage indeed. He was one of the gardeners and kept the grounds of the palace in good order.

Now just as he had nearly reached his home, with the imps close behind him, following quietly in his footsteps, someone came running to meet Grunts.

"The Queen wants you!" panted the messenger. "She wants some extra special roses for a dinner party tonight, and says will you please pick them now?"

"I'll go straight to the palace," said Grunts. So, instead of going home, he turned to the right and took the path

that led to the palace garden. The imps went too, for they thought they would like to see the roses.

Grunts went in at a little green gate, and picked the roses for the Queen. Just as he had finished gathering a beautiful bunch, Her Majesty came down the path.

"Oh thank you, Grunts," she said. "I'll take them in myself. Oh dear me, what's this?"

She had nearly fallen over the brown parcel in which the bellows were. Grunts had put it down on the grass while he picked the roses.

"I beg your pardon, Your Majesty," he said. "Those are my new bellows."

"Oh, could you lend me them for a moment?" asked the Queen. "The fire in the drawing-room wants a good blowing, and we can't find the bellows anywhere."

"Certainly, Your Majesty," said Grunts. "Pray let me come and do it for you."

He picked up the bellows, and walked down the path with the Queen. The two imps were full of horror. Oh dear, oh dear! Whatever would happen in the palace

when the bellows blew! They ran after the Queen and Grunts, meaning to beg them not to use the bellows.

But they were too late. Grunts was kneeling down by the fire, blowing hard with the bellows, when the two imps looked in at the window.

Then things began to happen. Suddenly a loud wheezing sound came from the bellows, and they leaped right out of Grunts' hands. They worked themselves, and a great wind came out of them. It blew all the roses out of the vase that the Queen had put them in. Then it blew all the newspapers out of the rack, and puffed the curtains right out of the window.

"Oh, oh!" cried the Queen. "Whatever

13

is happening? Take the bellows outside, Grunts! There is something wrong with them!"

But Grunts couldn't catch them! They went flying all over the place, blowing for all they were worth. *Puff-puff-puff*! And off went the cushions from the couch, and into the air went the table-cloth! The cat was blown right off her chair, and the dog sailed out of the room backwards. The Queen's hair was blown all about her face, and she had to hold tightly to the mantelpiece to prevent herself from being blown out of the window!

"Ooh!" cried Bubble and Squeak, as the bellows suddenly puffed at them. Off they went, blown backwards, rolling over and over. Then they sat up and looked at one another.

Bubble began to cry.

"I do wish we hadn't been naughty," he sobbed. "Look what's happened now! Whoever would have thought that the Blowaway Witch would have sold us such a strong spell for fivepence. And it's

getting stronger every minute!"

So it was. The bellows made a much louder noise now, and blew so strongly that even chairs and tables went rolling over. Then the bellows flew out into the hall, and met a footman carrying a tray of cups and plates.

Every single one was blown into the air, and came down in pieces. As for the poor footman, he was blown to the end of the hall, and knocked the King himself over.

"Now what's this, what's this?" cried the King in a temper. "What do you mean by tearing about backwards like this, footman?"

But just then the bellows came near and – *puff*! The King himself was blown into the air and bumped his head against the ceiling. He caught hold of a swinging lantern and hung there, very much frightened. The footman ran to get a ladder to help him down.

What a to-do there was in the palace! The King shouted, the Queen cried, the footman rushed here and there trying to

catch the bellows, and the cook threw a saucepan at them but only managed to hit the butler, who was very angry.

The bellows thoroughly enjoyed themselves. They sent a large bed sailing into the garden, and went out after it. Then they blew two chimney pots off the roof, and puffed so hard at a gardener that he found himself sitting at the top of a beech tree before he knew what was happening.

Grunts was filled with amazement. How could his pair of bellows be so wicked? Hadn't he bought them for a

17

halfpenny that day from Bubble and Squeak? Surely they couldn't have put such a strong spell into them?

As for Bubble and Squeak, they were shaking and trembling, for they knew that they would be found out and punished sooner or later. Whatever would the Queen say to them? And how could that dreadful pair of bellows be stopped?

"Let's run to the Blowaway Witch and ask her what to do!" said Bubble, with tears running down his turned-up nose. So off they went.

They didn't stop once till they reached the witch's cottage. Then they banged on her door.

When she came, they told her all that had happened.

"The King was blown up to the ceiling, and the gardener sailed up to the top of the beech tree, and all the cups and saucers and plates flew into the air off the footman's tray!" sobbed Bubble. "Oh, whatever are we to do? We didn't know you had given us such a strong wind-spell, witch. How can we stop it?"

The witch went very pale, and sat down suddenly.

"I didn't give you a strong spell," she said. "I gave you the weakest one I had, for I was afraid you were up to mischief, as usual. What can have happened to it?"

"Do you suppose the South Wind did anything to your spell?" asked Squeak. "He was here when you sold it to us, you know."

"So he was," said the witch, jumping up. "Well, I'll get him here, and ask him."

She took an old tea tray out to her garden, and banged it with a metal spoon.

In three minutes the South Wind came rushing down.

"What do you want?" he asked. "I heard you calling me."

The witch told him all that had happened at the palace, and the South Wind looked most uncomfortable.

"Yes," he said. "I breathed on the spell and made it very strong – very strong indeed – but of course I hadn't any idea at all that the Queen herself would ask for the bellows to be used in the palace. I thought perhaps some old gnome or goblin would get a shock, that's all."

"Well, what are we to do?" asked the imps.

"The South Wind and I will come with you and see if we can stop the bellows from blowing," said the witch. She put on her best cloak, climbed on her broomstick, took the two imps behind her, and then set off with the South Wind to the palace.

When they arrived there, they found the enchanted bellows still blowing everywhere. The King's crown had been blown to the top of a chimney, and six hens had been puffed up to the highest tower of the palace. It was dreadful.

The witch hastily drew a circle of white chalk, and stepped inside it. Then she chanted a long string of magic words, beckoning the bellows towards her all the time. Little by little they stopped blowing, and came towards the witch. As soon as they were near the magic circle, she reached out her hand and grabbed them. Once they were in the circle all

their enchantment left them, and they became ordinary bellows.

"Well, they're cured now," said the witch, and she stepped out of her circle. She went to the Queen and told her everything that had happened to make the bellows behave so strangely.

The King and Queen were very angry.

"The imps had no right to play tricks like that," they said, "and as for the South Wind, he ought to be ashamed of himself for his share in this terrible muddle. Just look at the palace! Everything is upside down and topsy-turvy! He shall be banished from Fairyland for a whole year, and he can take those mischievous imps with him!"

Very sorrowfully the South Wind went away, and the two imps followed him, weeping bitterly. The footman picked up the bellows and threw them after the imps – and as soon as they left the magic circle, their enchantment came back. They began to blow and blow again, and the two imps flew straight up into the air, and found themselves in the clouds.

The South Wind caught the bellows, and gave them to the imps.

"I will look after you and be your friend," he said, "but you must work for me in return. Sometimes I can't be bothered to blow the clouds along on a summer's day, because I'm too sleepy. You can blow them for me with these bellows."

And that is what Bubble and Squeak do now. If you see the clouds sailing slowly along on a summer's day when there is no breeze, you will be able to guess what is happening – the South Wind is fast asleep somewhere, and the two imps are puffing the clouds along with the bellows. They hope to go back to Fairyland some day, and if they are good, I expect they will.

The Garden
Party

"Mrs Barnley is organising a garden party soon," said Mother. "We must go to it. I wonder if I can help her. She'll be so very busy arranging everything."

"You're always helping everybody, Mummy," said Daisy. "I think you're the kindest person in the world. I do feel very proud of having you for a mother."

Mother laughed and kissed her. "Do you, Daisy?" she said. "Well, you know, I'd like you to be just the same, kind and helpful, so that I could feel you were the kindest twins in the world! It's very nice to feel proud of people, isn't it?"

The twins talked to one another about this when their mother had gone. "You know, we ought to try and help a bit more," said Daisy. "Can't we help at Mrs

Barnley's garden party too? Let's go and ask her if we can."

So off they went to her house. She was very pleased to see them. "Well, my dears, I want somebody who can give the children rides on a pony!" she said. "Can you do that?"

"We haven't got a pony," said Dan. "But I know what we could do instead – for the very little ones, Mrs Barnley. We could bring our tricycle and charge fivepence a ride down the long path if you like."

"Well, that would be a good idea!" said Mrs Barnley. So, on the afternoon of the party the twins took their tricycle, beautifully clean and shining, to the

garden party. Daisy had made a fine big card, with "Tricycle rides, fivepence" written on it.

How busy the twins were that afternoon, giving rides. They got hot and tired, but they didn't mind a bit. And do you know, when they counted up the fivepenny pieces they had in their bag, there were ninety-two!

"Four pounds and sixty pence!" said Mrs Barnley, delighted. "How wonderful, twins! Really, I don't know what I should have done without you and your mother. I'm proud of you all!"

And you can just imagine how proud the twins' mother was of Dan and Daisy!

The Nine
Wooden Soldiers

There were once nine wooden soldiers in a cardboard box. They were very proud of themselves, and each night when everyone was in bed, they climbed out of their box and went marching round the room.

One banged a tiny drum. One blew a tiny trumpet. The others shouldered their wooden guns and marched stiffly in a long line. All the toys watched them and thought they were fine.

"Nine wooden soldiers, nine,
Marching along in a line,
Nobody else is half so fine
As the nine wooden soldiers, nine!"

sang the soldiers, in time to the drum and the trumpet.

Now one evening as they climbed out of

their box, the trumpeter happened to count them – and he only counted eight! How strange! He counted them once again – one, two, three, four, five, six, seven, eight!

"One of us is missing!" he cried. "Who is it? There are only eight of us!"

"I will count us," said the drummer, and he counted slowly, pointing to each soldier in turn, "One, two, three, four, five, six, seven, eight! Yes – there are only eight of us!"

The soldiers were dreadfully worried. What had happened to the ninth soldier? They stared at one another and tried to see who was missing – but everyone seemed to be there. It was very strange. They could not march along, singing their song about nine wooden soldiers, nine, if there were only eight of them!

They counted once more – yes, there seemed to be only eight. But, oh, the silly little soldiers, they had each forgotten something when they had counted. Each soldier had forgotten to count himself! He had pointed to all the others, but not to his own little wooden self. So no wonder he only counted eight.

Whilst they were standing talking and worrying, the old, ragged toy dog came up. He was so old and dirty and ragged that none of the other toys liked him near them. They wouldn't even let him sleep in the toy cupboard with them. But he was a kind old thing, and he wondered why the soldiers did not start out on their usual march round the room.

"Well, you see, ragged dog, one of us is lost," said the drummer. "There are only eight of us, look!"

He counted, pointing with his finger to each soldier – and again he missed out himself! How the ragged dog laughed!

"Now, you watch me count!" he said. "There are nine of you all right. Listen! One-two-three-four-five-six-seven-eight-nine! There you are – nine wooden soldiers, nine!"

"So we are!" said the soldiers, in wonder and delight. "Oh, ragged dog, you have made us so happy. There is not any-one missing, after all. You do count well. What can we do for you in return for making us so happy?"

"Let me sleep in your box with you," begged the ragged dog. "The toys turn me out of the cupboard at night, and I am lonely."

"Of course you shall sleep in our box!" cried all the soldiers in delight. "We'd love to have a clever dog like you living with us!"

Then off they went again round the floor, the drummer drumming, the trumpeter trumpeting, and all the rest singing loudly:

"Nine wooden soldiers, nine,
Marching along in a line,
Nobody else is half so fine
As the nine wooden soldiers, nine!"

And behind them marched the old ragged dog, wagging his tail and wuffing for all he was worth!

Go Away,
Black Cat!

The black cat was a great nuisance in the nursery. He wasn't very large and he didn't make any noise – but he would keep getting out the farmyard animals and playing with them!

He sent them sliding all round the floor with his paw, and then pounced after them. The animals were made of wood, so he couldn't really hurt them, but they didn't like being slid all over the place like that.

"Go away, black cat!" said the pink pig from the farmyard.

"Go away, black cat!" mooed the cow, who was a little bit afraid of having her long tail broken.

"Oh, go away, black cat!" scolded the sheep, who was very tired of being smacked all over the room, just to please the cat.

The black cat said nothing. He didn't even miaow. He only came in because he loved to play with the little toys, and send them hopping about the room. It was fun to hear them shouting at him too, and not take any notice.

"I wish we could stop him!" said the toy farmer, who was always afraid he might be sent sliding over the floor too. He usually hurried into his farmhouse when he saw the black cat, but he knew quite well that the cat could put his paw into the farmhouse and get him out if he wished!

"I know – I know what we can do!" squeaked a tiny little doll dressed as a sailor. He sat in a small wooden boat, and

was cross because the others didn't take much notice of him.

"Oh, you be quiet," said the bear. "You're always talking."

"But I know what to do!" cried the sailor-doll.

"No, you don't," the toy rabbit said rudely. "Be quiet! How could a tiny thing like you know better than big toys like us?"

The sailor-doll sulked and said no more. The red-haired doll thought it would be a good idea to let the three toy dogs bark at the black cat and frighten him. So the black dog, the white dog, and the pink dog were all arranged in a row in front of the farmyard, ready to bark.

How they barked when the black cat appeared! "Wuff, wuff! Go away, black cat! Wuff, wuff! Go away, black cat!"

The black cat looked at them and grinned till his mouth nearly reached his ears. Then he began to play with the toy dogs! He sent them here and he sent them there; he threw them into the air – he had a lovely time!

But the dogs didn't. They were very angry. When the black cat had gone, the tiny sailor-doll spoke again.

"I know what to do, I know what – "

"Be quiet!" shouted the bear. "Toys, I've got a fine idea! Let's stand by the door with a pail of water and empty it over the cat when he comes in!"

So they filled a little seaside pail with water and waited by the door. But the black cat jumped in at the window and when he saw the bear and the rabbit waiting with their pail of water, he ran to them, and tipped up the pail so that the water wetted their feet! Then he played with the farmyard animals and broke the leg of one of the pigs.

The sailor-doll didn't say any more. He went to the Noah's ark and lifted up the lid. "Noah!" he said. "Take your animals for a walk round the room. It will do them good."

So Noah took all his animals two by two round the room, and the sailor-doll waited patiently by the ark. Soon the black cat peeped in at the door, and the sailor-doll began to behave in a very peculiar manner.

He began to scrape inside the ark as if he had gone mad, and he shouted out, "A mouse! A mouse! You naughty mouse, come out of the ark! You have frightened away Noah and all his animals!"

The black cat pricked up his ears at the word "mouse". He saw Noah and the animals walking round the room, and he sprang to the ark to find the mouse.

"Get in and catch it! Get in and catch it!" cried the sailor-doll, and the cat jumped right inside the big wooden ark.

Slam! The sailor-doll shut down the lid with a bang, and yelled to the other toys, "Come and help me. Put something on top, quick! Come and put something on top!"

They all rushed to the ark, carrying many different things. The rabbit carried a stool. The red-haired doll carried a big top. The bear brought two books. Everybody brought something.

Bang! Bang! Bang! Everything was slammed down on to the lid of the ark. More books were fetched, and somehow

or other the rabbit and the bear eventually managed to balance the sailor-doll's little wooden boat on the Noah's ark, too, to keep down the lid.

The black cat banged his head against the lid trying to get out. He had seen at once that there was no mouse there, and now he was very frightened. Suppose he never got out of this dreadful, dark wooden place that smelled of the Noah's ark animals!

"Let-me-ow-out!" he mewed. "Let-me-ow-out!"

"Well, do you promise never, never to come into our room again?" cried the sailor-doll boldly. "If you do come again, I'll lock you into a brick-box and put it at the bottom of the cupboard where nobody will find it!"

"Oh, ow! Oh, ow!" wailed the black cat. "Don't do that! I'll never, never come here again! Let-me-ow-out!"

The sailor-doll chuckled to himself. He cried out loudly, "Well – one, two, three – out you come!" He upset all the things on the lid and they crashed to the floor. The

black cat lifted up the lid with his head and jumped out. His ears were set back, his tail was standing straight up – he was very, very frightened!

He tore out of the room at top speed, yowling loudly. The sailor-doll chuckled. "You can come back, Noah!" he shouted to Noah and the animals. Then he turned to the watching toys, who all looked pleased and astonished.

"Now maybe you see that you should listen to me whenever I begin to talk!" he said. "Do you understand?"

"Yes, Sailor-Doll!" answered all the toys, most politely. And now I expect that the sailor-doll will talk all day long – don't you?

39

The Very
Forgetful Gnome

One day Twiddle the enchanter heard of a marvellous broom. His friend, Mother Doodah, told him of it.

"It's really wonderful!" she said. "This broom, if stood just outside your door, Twiddle, knows at once if an enemy is coming to see you. When the enemy is just about to knock at the door the broom rushes out from its corner and sweeps him right down the garden path into the nearest puddle."

"What a marvellous thing!" said Twiddle, who had a great many enemies and was often bothered by them. "I really think I must get that broom. It would be most useful to me. Who has it now, Mother Doodah?"

"The gnome, Mister Dithery, has it, I

think," said Mother Doodah. "He has had it for about fifty years, so people say. If it isn't worn out by now you could probably buy it from him."

"I'll certainly try!" cried Twiddle, and he put on his best cloak and tallest hat at once. With him he carried a leather bag in which he had put twenty gold pieces. He thought he would have to pay highly for such a marvellous broom.

Dithery the gnome lived in a crooked house at the end of Humpty Village. Twiddle soon found it when he asked his way, and he strode up the path to the yellow front door, jingling all his money in his bag.

Blim-blam! He knocked loudly.

"Put the potatoes down on the step!" cried a husky voice from inside. "I'm busy."

"I haven't brought any potatoes!" the enchanter shouted indignantly. "Open the door."

"I tell you, I'm busy!" said the voice, crossly. "If you are the washing, just leave it till next week."

"I'm not the washing either!" shouted Twiddle, stamping his foot. "I'm Twiddle the enchanter and I've come to buy something from you."

"Oh! Well, why didn't you say so before?" said the husky voice. There came the *thud-thud* of big feet and the door was opened. Twiddle stepped inside. Dithery was a strange-looking gnome. His head was enormous, and he had a curious beard, which was neatly parted in two and tied up with blue ribbons.

"Good morning," said Twiddle, looking all round. "I've come to buy your broom. You know – the magic one that sweeps up enemies."

"Oh, that one!" said Dithery, rubbing his long nose. "Well, now, I haven't seen it for a very long time. I wonder what I did with it."

"Don't you use it?" asked Twiddle in great surprise.

"Oh, no, not now," said the gnome. "Not for a good many years. You see, people got so afraid of being swept up that everybody decided to be friends with me. So the broom was no longer any use for sweeping up my enemies, and I used it for an ordinary broom. It was fine for sweeping up the yard."

"Fancy using a magic broom for yard rubbish," said the enchanter, in horror. "You don't deserve to have anything valuable, Dithery, really you don't! Tell me where the broom is."

"What are you going to give me for it?" asked Dithery, twisting his beard round his fingers and messing up his nice blue ribbons.

"Well, I've brought a very large price for it," said Twiddle, jingling his leather bag. "Twenty whole golden pieces."

"Ooh!" said Dithery, his eyes opening wide. "That's fine. Give them to me, please. I want to buy a horse for myself. There's a lovely one for sale in our village."

Twiddle counted out the money into Dithery's horny hand. The gnome went to the door and whistled. A small pixie came running up. The gnome gave him the twenty gold pieces and told him to go at once and buy the blue-spotted horse that Mister Ho-Ho had for sale.

"And bring it back to me this morning," he ordered. The pixie ran off down the road.

"Now, Dithery, just tell me where the magic broom is, quickly!" said Twiddle impatiently. He had been looking all round, but he couldn't see it anywhere.

"Let me see now," said Dithery, thinking so hard that his head swelled up like a balloon. "You might look under the sink there. That's a likely place for it."

Twiddle looked under the sink. To his surprise there were four little folding tables neatly stacked there, one against another.

"There's no broom here, Dithery," he said. "There are only a lot of little folding tables."

"Dear me, so that's where I put those tables," said Dithery. "I wondered where they were. I got them for a party I was going to have, and then lost the tables. So I couldn't have the party."

Twiddle looked at him in astonishment. Fancy forgetting things like that!

"Well, where else do you think the broom might be?" he asked.

"Let me think," said Dithery. "Oh yes – it might be in that cupboard over there. I'm sure I put it there, Twiddle."

Twiddle opened the cupboard door, and out fell a great collection of cardboard boxes of all sizes. *Crash, crash!* They fell on his head and made him jump terribly.

Dithery began to laugh. "Oh, dear," he said. "I'm really very sorry about that, Twiddle. I quite forgot I had emptied that cupboard to make room for my boxes. I always save every box I get, you know, just in case I want one for anything. I needed one yesterday and couldn't find them anywhere – so I'm pleased to know where they are."

"Whatever's the good of saving them if you forget where you've put them?" said Twiddle in disgust, kicking them back into the cupboard and slamming the door. "Well, where did you put the things you turned out of this cupboard, Dithery? Do try and think."

"All right," said Dithery, screwing up his face. "Yes – I put them all in the oven. There didn't seem to be room anywhere else."

"In the oven?" said Twiddle, staring in amazement at the gnome. "Are you mad, Dithery? Whatever made you put them in the *oven*?"

Twiddle went to the stove and pulled open the oven door. Inside lay a mass of half-burnt things – blackened brushes, a broken dustpan, a lot of useless tins of polish.

"Goodness!" said Dithery, looking at them as the enchanter raked them all out. "So that's what that terrible smell was last month. I couldn't think what it could be! I suppose all those things got cooked when I lit the fire."

Twiddle thought of quite a lot of things to say but they were all too rude, so he didn't say anything at all, but just thought that Dithery was the stupidest gnome he had ever come across. He poked about among the half-burnt things, but to his delight there was no broom there. He had been very much afraid that he would find it burnt so that it would be of no use at all – but it wasn't there.

"Dithery, think again," he said at last. "The broom isn't in the oven."

"Oh yes, I remember now," said Dithery, cheering up. "I put it in . . . oh! Look! There's my new horse!"

There was a sound of clip-clopping hoofs and a horse looked in at the door.

Twiddle thought it was a most peculiar creature, not at all worth twenty golden pieces. It was covered with bright blue spots, and wore spectacles and a hat tied up with a yellow ribbon.

"Brrrooomph!" said the odd-looking horse, politely.

"Oh, you darling!" cried Dithery, dancing up to it. "I'll go for a ride on you straight away!"

He was just going to climb up on the horse's back when Twiddle caught hold of his legs and pulled him firmly away.

49

"No," he said, "no, Dithery! You will not go for a ride. You will not do anything until you have found me that magic broom. Go out, horse!"

"Brrrooomph!" said the horse, in disappointment, and out it went. It sat down on a seat in the garden. Twiddle thought it was the strangest horse he had ever seen.

"Now, Dithery, think again and tell me where that broom is," he said.

Dithery's head swelled up once more, which showed Twiddle that he was really thinking.

"I might have put it in the dog-kennel," he said at last, in his husky voice.

"The dog-kennel!" said Twiddle, in astonishment. "Whatever for?"

"Well, I must have somewhere to put things, mustn't I?" said Dithery, rather sulkily. "I often put things into the dog-kennel. There's no dog there, and the kennel would be wasted if I didn't use it for something!"

Twiddle went into the yard where a big dog-kennel stood in one corner. He

looked inside. To his enormous surprise itwas full of potatoes!

"Dithery! This dog-kennel is full of potatoes!" cried Twiddle.

"Oh my, of course! I did put the potatoes there," said Dithery, running out. "I quite forgot. No wonder I couldn't find them when I looked in the vegetable rack. Now I shall be able to have potatoes for my dinner again."

"Dithery, will you please think where the broom is," begged Twiddle, who was beginning to feel he was in a most annoying sort of dream. "Do remember!"

"Well, I keep remembering!" replied Dithery, most indignantly. "I've remembered all sorts of places."

"But not the right ones," said Twiddle, patiently. "Just remember the right one, now."

"Well – you might look in the kitchen cupboard on the top shelf," said Dithery. "I often put things there out of the way."

Twiddle thought it was a funny sort of place to put a broom, but he went to the cupboard door and opened it. He looked on the top shelf, but all he could see on it was a large round tin. He opened it – and found a bright yellow coat!

"Dithery! There's no broom here – only a round tin and inside it is a yellow coat! Whatever made you put a yellow coat here?"

"Ooh!" squeaked Dithery in delight. "So that's where I put my yellow coat. I wondered where it could be! It's my best one. Pass it to me, Twiddle. I've had to wear my old one for a long time now. Oh, I remember – I put it there because my wardrobe was so full of other things."

Twiddle snorted angrily and threw the coat to Dithery. He was delighted to have his best coat back.

"What was your wardrobe so full of that you couldn't even put your coat there?" Twiddle asked. "I suppose you keep your coal there, or something like that?"

"Well, yes, I believe my coal is there," said Dithery. He walked into his bedroom and opened the door of the wardrobe – but it wasn't full of coal after all. It was simply crammed with fishing-nets!

"Must you keep fishing-nets in your wardrobe?" asked Twiddle, in a tired sort of voice. "People don't usually, you know. Whatever made you get so many nets, anyway?"

"Oh, somebody said there was a big fish in the village pond," said Dithery. "So I bought those nets to catch it. But I forgot where I'd put them. I should have caught that fish easily if only I'd had my nets, I know I should."

"Where did you put the things you took out of the wardrobe when you put the nets in?" asked Twiddle, feeling that he really would like to pinch Dithery, or slap him, or do something really horrid to him. He was the most annoying person that Twiddle had ever met.

"Let me see," said Dithery. "I kept my garden tools there, I think – so the broom might have been among them. Now where did I put them?"

A piece of coal fell out of the fire while he was thinking and Dithery bent to sweep up the mess. He took up a flat broom-head that stood on the hearth – and then he gave a loud yell that made Twiddle jump nearly out of his skin.

"Here's the broom!" he cried. "Of course! I quite forgot I'd been using it for the fire. I took off the handle and just used the broom-head. It is very good for sweeping up ashes."

Twiddle stared at the old, dirty, blackened broom-head in horror.

"Do you mean to say that you took off the handle and used a valuable magic broom to sweep up ashes?" he said sternly.

"Well, it wasn't much use for anything else," said the gnome, sulkily. "I haven't any enemies at all now."

"You'll make an enemy of me if you go on like this," said Twiddle, fiercely. "I've wasted all my morning looking in stupid places for that broom, and finding all kinds of silly things for you, and the broom was there under my nose all the time. Now where's the handle?"

"I really can't imagine," said Dithery, cheerfully.

Twiddle went almost mad with rage. He bent down and shouted in Dithery's ear.

"Tell me where that handle is or I'll turn you into a box of matches and strike you till you're all used up!" he yelled.

"This broom is no use without its handle."

"Don't get cross with me or I shan't be able to remember anything at all," said Dithery, sulking.

"Well, you haven't remembered anything of any use so far," said Twiddle, gloomily.

"I think I know where the handle is," said Dithery, suddenly. "Yes, I do! I made a bird-table, and used the handle for a pole to put the tray-piece of the table on, to put it out of reach of cats, you know."

"What! You used the handle of a magic broom to make a bird-table!" cried Twiddle, horrified. "Well, you don't deserve to have anything valuable at all. You really don't."

He looked out into the garden for the bird-table, but he couldn't see one anywhere.

"I suppose you've tied the bird-table to the chimney or done something just as silly," he grumbled. "Where is it, Dithery?"

"It's under my bed," said Dithery. "I

put it there, I know, but I can't remember why, now."

"Probably because you wanted to make things really difficult for the birds!" said Twiddle, shaking his head in wonder at Dithery's brains. "All right – I'll get it."

He went into the bedroom and looked under the bed – and wonder of wonders, the bird-table really was there! Its broom-handle leg stuck out, and it wasn't many seconds before Twiddle had it in his hand. Now he had both the broom-head and the broom-handle. Good! At last he could go home.

He fitted the head to the handle and made a proper broom. Dithery watched him.

"There you are!" he said. "Now you've got the old broom, you see – and I'm going to go for a ride on my nice new horse. Goodbye!"

He ran out into the garden, and the horse stood up. "Brrrooomph!" he went. "Brrrooomph!"

Dithery jumped up on to his back, and off they galloped down the path, the

horse's spectacles jerking up and down on his big nose.

Twiddle put the broom over his shoulder and walked down the path and out of the gate, delighted to have the magic broom at last. He walked down the street and as he passed a little twisted cottage, with twelve tall chimneys rising from its roof, someone called him.

"Hi! Road-sweeper! Will you come and sweep my path for me? It's very untidy with all the fallen leaves."

"I'm not a road-sweeper," said Twiddle, indignantly.

"Well, that's a road-sweeping broom, isn't it?" asked the little person in surprise, leaning out of her window to look.

"Indeed it's not!" said Twiddle. "It's a very magic broom indeed. It once belonged to Dithery the gnome, and he has sold it to me this morning for twenty golden pieces."

The little pixie-like person stared at Twiddle in surprise, and then she began to laugh very loudly indeed.

"Ho-ho, he-he!" she giggled. "You don't mean to say that you've paid Dithery twenty golden pieces for that old broom over your shoulder? Why, that's not the magic broom! He sold that to my aunt five years ago, but I expect he's forgotten all about it by now. He's a marvellous forgetter, you know! Oh, what a joke! Where is Dithery now? You'd better go and get back your money."

"He bought a blue-spotted horse and has gone riding on it," said Twiddle, in a great rage. He flung the broom down on the ground and snorted so angrily that

the little pixie woman looked quite alarmed.

"Oh, so he's bought that horse, has he?" she said. "Well, it's no good waiting for him to come back, then. He's gone to visit his Aunt Dumpling, a thing he's been waiting to do for years and years. Only a blue-spotted horse knows the way, and he's been longing to buy one. He won't be back for at least a year."

"Where does your aunt live?" asked Twiddle, gloomily. "I suppose I'll have to go and buy the magic broom from her. All I hope is that she's got a better memory than Dithery the gnome has."

"Oh yes," said the little pixie person.

"She keeps the magic broom on her front doorstep and it sweeps up all her enemies nicely. You'd better take that frown off your face before you call on her or else the broom will think you're an enemy and will sweep you up!"

Off went poor Twiddle to buy the broom. He really did buy it, this time, and took it home with him. It swept up all his enemies beautifully. He has just heard that Dithery the gnome has come back from his visit to his aunt – and has sent him a note asking him to come and see him.

"He's my enemy!" he has told the broom, fiercely. "So mind you sweep him up very roughly indeed, and land him *splash*! in the biggest puddle there is!"

But I don't expect old Dithery will remember to go and call on Twiddle, do you?

That Girl
Next Door!

Dick, Juliet and Robert loved the girl next door, but their mother didn't.

"I never knew such a tomboy!" she said. "Always climbing trees and tearing her clothes and shouting and playing cowboys and Indians and goodness knows what!"

"But, Mum, she's fun," said Dick. "Anyway, she hasn't got a mother to tell her not to, poor thing."

"Tessa's nice," said Juliet. "She's kind."

"I like playing with her," said Robert.

"Well – I suppose there's no harm in her," said their mother. "But she is so noisy! And she always looks such a little mess. Still, having no mother does make things difficult. She's got no one to teach her to be clean and good mannered."

The three children lived near the wide River Thames. Their father had a boat but he wouldn't let them go in it unless he was there. For one thing his children couldn't swim, and he was afraid they might fall into the water.

Tessa could swim like a fish. She said she had taught herself. She could row a boat, too, though her father hadn't got one of his own. In fact, or so the children thought, Tessa could do anything!

One day the children's mother had to go and see her sister, who was ill.

"Now I shall have to leave you three alone for a little while," she said. "I hope that girl next door doesn't come in and lead you into mischief. But I think she's out. Now, just be good children while I'm gone."

And off she went. She hadn't been gone for more than five minutes when Tessa came to the fence and gave her loud call. "Coo-eeee!"

"It's Tessa!" said the three children and ran eagerly into the garden.

"Hello," said Tessa. "Shall we play?

Will your mother mind if I come into your garden?"

"She's out," said Dick. "Come in, Tessa. We can play one of your 'let's pretend' games."

"Ooooh, yes," said Juliet and Robert. Tessa was marvellous at "let's pretend". She could be a most lifelike cowboy, or shipwrecked sailor, or pirate or policeman or burglar. It really was exciting when she played.

"I know what we'll play today," said Tessa, climbing over the wall. "Let's play shipwrecked sailors."

"Oh, yes. How do you play it?" said Juliet.

"Well, we want a desert island to be wrecked on – that round bit of grass will do," said Tessa, and the bit of grass immediately looked like a desert island. "And we want a raft to get away on."

"A raft?" echoed the others. "How can we make a raft?"

Tessa knew how to make a raft, of course. "You know that old kitchen table of yours?" she said. "Well, that will make a wonderful raft – upside down, you know, with a white flag flying from one of the legs as a signal to our rescuers."

This all sounded very exciting – but Dick didn't know whether his mother would like them to use her old kitchen table. "Oh, don't be silly," said Tessa, "we're not going to damage it! I'll help you to bring it out."

Well, it wasn't long before the game was going well. They were all truly shipwrecked on the desert island – and then Tessa pretended to build the raft. She even borrowed a hammer from the

toolbox and hammered at the raft as if she really was making it. Everything she did was so real.

"Now we must tie a flag to one of the legs," she said. "What about that white cloth on your line? That's just the right size."

The white cloth was tied to the leg.

"Now we want a paddle," said Tessa. "Get one of your spades – the biggest one. I'll do the paddling. What a pity this

67

is all pretence! If only we could float away on the river!"

It was a lovely game. They all got on the upside-down table and Tessa paddled valiantly, telling them to keep their eyes open for a rescue boat. It was when Juliet was shading her eyes, looking for a rescue boat, that she suddenly saw something that frightened her.

"Tessa – stop! I saw somebody falling in the river," she said, clutching Tessa's arm. "You know that little boy who lives on the other side of the river? It was him. I'm sure it was!"

They all gazed over the river. Then they heard a scream. They saw something being washed into midstream, and the three children were in a panic.

But not Tessa. She knew what to do at once. She jumped out of the table-raft and yelled to the others. "Help me to carry it to the river, come on, quick! This is as good as a boat. I'll go after the little boy."

The children were too dazed not to obey. They half-ran with the upside-down table through the gate to the river, and Tessa launched it on the water, jumping in herself with the little spade for a paddle.

The table was wood and floated well. Tessa began to paddle fast with the little spade, her eyes on the bundle of clothes that was the little boy from across the river. That was all he looked like as he floated along – just a bunch of clothes.

The current was taking him out to midstream. Tessa paddled manfully. She got nearer and nearer. The boy bobbed close, and she sat down, clutched a table leg and grabbed at the boy's shirt as he bobbed nearer still. She got hold of him!

But she couldn't pull him on the table-raft because every time she tried the table almost turned over. Tessa wondered what to do. Then she saw that a boat was coming swiftly near. Someone else had seen what had happened.

A man dived in and came up near the child. He took him from Tessa and life-saved him, swimming strongly with the child's face uppermost. Willing hands

dragged them both aboard the little boat and rowed back to the child's home on the opposite side.

"Well done, thank you!" a voice called to her from the boat. Tessa waved and then paddled her raft back to shore. And there, on the bank, was the children's mother, home from her visit! The children had told her what was happening, and she was waiting there for Tessa.

"Oh dear!" thought Tessa. "Now I shall get into trouble for taking the table out on the water!"

But she didn't! The children's mother kissed her and praised her. "You saved that boy's life!" she said. "You're a fine girl, Tessa. How proud your mother would have been of you. Now don't look as if I'm going to scold you for going off with my table – I'm not. Shall we make a bargain, Tessa?"

"What bargain?" asked Tessa, slipping her hand into the hand of the children's mother.

"You let me teach you how to sew and speak nicely and learn good manners as

Dick, Juliet and Robert do," said their mother. "And in return will you teach my three how to swim and how to row and run and jump like you do?"

"Will you be like a mother?" asked Tessa, delighted. "I always wanted a real mother."

"I will," said the children's mother. "I'll have four children instead of three! And now come along and have a very special tea on that wonderful old kitchen table. Little did it know it was to be a raft some day and go floating on the water!"

When the other three can swim they're planning to go out on that table together. I only hope it will bear their weight – but still, as Tessa says, what does it matter if it sinks? They'll simply be shipwrecked sailors swimming to the shore!

Annabel's Nest

"The birds are all making their nests," said Annabel. "Look, Mummy, there's a sparrow with a feather in his beak. He's taking it to tuck into his nest somewhere, isn't he?"

"I expect so," said her mother. "And there's another bird with a straw, Annabel. They are all very busy with their nests just now!"

"How can they make them if they haven't any hands?" said Annabel. "They only have their beaks. They don't use their feet to build nests with, do they?"

"Oh, no," said her mother. "Only their beaks. They are very clever with them. They tuck the bits and pieces in here and there, and make the lovely nests you see in the hedges. It is a great shame when somebody pulls a nest to pieces, because it takes a bird quite a long time to build its beautiful little nest."

"I shall make one myself," said Annabel. "I ought to be able to make a very, very good one, because I have two hands, with fingers and thumbs. Now let me see, what do I want for a nest?"

"Little twigs, bits of hay, root fibres, moss, dead leaves, hair, feathers – things like that," said her mother.

"I'll make a lovely nest," said Annabel. "And I'll put it in the middle of the hawthorn hedge, and then if any bird has its own nest spoilt it can have mine. I'm sure all the birds will see me making it and will know it is for any of them that needs a new nest."

She went out into the garden. She found plenty of tiny twigs, and she took some of the heather stems, because they were nice and thin and wiry – easy to weave together for a nest.

She found it much more difficult than she had thought it would be. "The little bits won't stay together," she said. "They

won't make a nice round nest. It looks untidy. I believe that one beak is better than two hands after all!"

Still, it did begin to look like a nest after a bit. Annabel stuffed some dead leaves into the cracks and trimmed it up with moss. It began to look very nice.

"How do I make it nice and round and cup-shaped inside?" she asked her mother. "What does the bird do to make it like a cup inside?"

"Oh, it just gets in and turns itself round and round a little," said Mother. "It soon becomes cup-shaped then."

Annabel put her little fist gently into

the nest and turned it round a little. "It's making a nice round place inside!" she cried. "Look – just like a real nest, Mummy!"

"It looks lovely," said Mother. "I think you have made it very well, Annabel."

"Oh, I do wish some bird would come and lay eggs in my nest," said Annabel. "Do you think one will?"

"I shouldn't think so," said her mother. "Birds like to make their own nests, you know."

No bird came to live in Annabel's nest, though two or three sparrows, a robin and a thrush came and had a good look at it. Annabel was disappointed. Her nest stayed in the hawthorn hedge, quite empty.

Then one day she came rushing to her mother. "Mummy! A dreadful thing's happened! You know the nest the robins made by the bank at the bottom of the garden – the one quite near the hedge where I put my nest? Well, somebody or something has pulled the robins' nest all to pieces – and oh, Mummy, the eggs are gone too. The little robins are dreadfully unhappy."

"Oh, dear," said her mother. "Surely no child has been cruel and destructive enough to pull a robins' nest to pieces. It must have been done by a rat who was after the eggs!"

She went down the garden with Annabel. Sure enough, there was the poor little nest, all pulled to pieces and scattered everywhere. There was no sign of the four red-brown eggs that the little robins had been so proud of.

"Look at the poor robins," said Annabel, crying. "They simply don't know what to do! They keep flying round and calling out – they don't know where to look for their eggs."

"The rat has eaten them," said her mother, sadly. "I'm afraid it was a rat."

"Will the robins use my nest now?" said Annabel, wiping her eyes.

"I shouldn't think so," said Mother. "You see, robins like to build somewhere low down – not high up in a hedge."

"I shall watch and see," said Annabel. So she stayed to watch – and that afternoon she suddenly began to feel excited. The robins flew up into the hedge and looked at the nest she had made.

"I believe they're going to have it for their new one!" thought the little girl. "I do believe they are. Then they will lay eggs in it and I shall have baby birds in my very own nest."

But to her great disappointment, they didn't use her nest. Instead they began to pull it to pieces. Annabel was surprised and sad.

"Oh! They knew how sad they were when they had their own nest pulled to bits – and now they're pulling mine to bits!" thought the little girl. "They're horrid!"

She ran to tell her mother. Mother came down the garden to see. Then she turned to Annabel with a smile.

"Annabel," she said, "they are certainly pulling your nest to pieces – but they are going to use all the bits to make another nest for themselves! What do you think of that? See, they are flying down to the ditch below the hawthorn hedge, with twigs and leaves in their mouths. They are saving themselves the trouble of hunting for nesting material! They are going to use all the stuff you collected!"

And that is exactly what the little red-breasted couple did do! They used Annabel's twigs and heather stems, and leaves and moss, and hair and feathers, for a perfectly new nest just below the hedge. Annabel was so pleased. She stayed and watched them all the time and they didn't mind a bit.

Now they have laid four more eggs in their new nest, and they always seem very pleased indeed when Annabel comes to have a look.

"She won't hurt us," they sing to one another. "She found all the stuff for this nest. She's a friend, a friend, a friend!"

You could build a nest too – just in case it might be useful!

The
Rascally Goblin

Once upon a time there was a little boy called Jack. He was a wonderful gardener, and you should have seen his flowers and vegetables! His sweetpeas were simply marvellous, and as for his lettuces and beans, Mother said they were better than she could buy in any shop!

For his birthday his father gave him a set of garden tools. Jack was delighted!

"They are really good ones, Jack," said his father, "so you must take great care of them. They are not cheap little ones like those you had before. Remember that whenever you use your tools, you must clean them well before putting them away, and you must always hang them up properly in the shed, and not leave them out in the garden."

"Oh yes, Daddy, I'll easily remember that," said Jack. "I do like good tools, and I'll keep them just as bright and shining as you keep yours!"

He did. He cleaned them well each night, and hung them up neatly on pegs in the shed.

And then strange things began to happen. Jack simply couldn't understand it. One morning he went to get his spade and it wasn't hanging up by the handle on its nail – it was lying down, and was as dirty as could be!

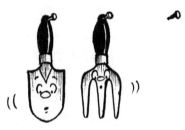

"Well, I am quite sure I cleaned it last night!" said Jack, puzzled. "But I must have forgotten to do it, I suppose!"

The next day when he went to get his watering-can it wasn't in the shed at all! Jack hunted for it, and at last found it out in the garden. How funny! He was sure he had put it into the shed when he had last used it.

Then there came a Saturday morning, and Father was at home to do some gardening too – and do you know, when he went with Jack to the shed to get his tools, he saw all Jack's new tools lying about anyhow in the shed, each of them dirty! He looked at them in surprise.

He was very cross with Jack. "Didn't you promise me that you would look after these beautiful new tools?" he said to Jack. "I am disappointed in you, Jack."

"But, Daddy, I did clean them and put them away," said Jack.

His father frowned. "Now, don't tell stories," he said. "It's bad enough to break a promise without telling untruths as well!"

Jack did not say any more. But he was very upset. He worked with his father all the morning, and when they stopped he was careful to clean his tools and hang them up nicely.

"That's right, Jack," said Father. "Now, listen – if I find those nice new tools lying about dirty again, I shall take them away, and you will have to use your old ones instead!"

Poor Jack! He knew that he always did put his tools away properly. He couldn't think how it was that they became dirty.

But the tools knew! When they were safely in the shed at night they talked to one another.

"It's a shame that Jack is blamed for what that rascally goblin does!" said the watering-can.

"Yes," said the spade, swinging to and fro on its nail. "He comes along and borrows us at night for his gardening, and never thinks of cleaning us or hanging us up properly."

"He's a horrid, nasty fellow," said the little fork. "He bent me the other day."

"And he loaded me so full that I thought my wheel would break!" said the barrow.

"I say! Won't it be horrid if Jack's father does take us away from him, and makes him use his old tools instead," said the trowel. "We shall be stuck away somewhere then, and never see the sunshine! Besides, I do like being used by Jack. He does make his garden so fine with us!"

"I've got an idea!" said the wheel-barrow thoughtfully. "Listen! I guess that rascally goblin will come along tonight. Well – let's be ready for him, shall we?"

"Ready for him? What do you mean?" asked the spade.

"Well – let's go for him and give him such a fright that he won't ever come here again!" said the barrow.

"Oooh, yes!" said the trowel. "That would be fine. I don't mind banging him on the head!"

"And I'd love to soak him with water!" said the watering-can, tilting itself up in glee.

"And I could run at him and run my wheel over his toes!" said the barrow, giving a great gurgle of laughter.

So it was all arranged. The tools got a come-alive spell from the little fairy they knew and they came alive for one night! The watering-can popped outside on spindly legs and filled itself at the tap! The spade hopped to the garden beds and filled itself full of earth. The barrow filled itself full of potatoes from a sack in the shed. The fork and the trowel practised jumping down from their nails, so that they might be ready when the great moment came!

Even the hosepipe joined in and said it would pretend to be a big snake! Oh dear! What fun they were going to have!

"Shh! Shh! Here comes the rascally goblin!" said the barrow suddenly. The shed-door opened and an ugly little head, with big pointed ears, looked in. Then the goblin ran inside and looked round for the tools.

"Where are you, spade? Where are you, barrow?" he said. "I've got a lot of digging to do tonight and a lot of watering too!"

"Here I am!" said the spade, and jumping up from the floor, where it had been lying ready with its spadeful of earth, it shot the earth all over the surprised goblin!

"Oooh! What's that?" said the goblin, alarmed.

The trowel jumped off its nail and hit him on the head, and the fork jumped too, and pricked him on the leg. The goblin scrambled up and ran for the door.

But the hosepipe was there, wriggling about like a big green snake!

"Oooh! Ow! Snakes!" yelled the frightened goblin. "Get away, snakes!"

But the hosepipe was thoroughly enjoying itself. It wriggled along after the goblin, and wound itself round his leg. The barrow laughed so much that it could hardly stand! Then it suddenly ran at the goblin, wheeled itself over his toe, and emptied all the potatoes over him. *Plop*, *thud*, *bang*, *crash*! How astonished that goblin was! He sat among the potatoes and yelled for help – but there was no one to hear him.

Then along came the watering-can, and lifted itself up into the air. *Pitter-patter, pitter-patter*! The water poured all over the goblin as the can watered him well! He ran to a corner, but the can followed him and soaked him wherever he went.

The hosepipe laughed so much that it forgot to be a snake by the door and the goblin tore out of the shed and made for home. He was wet and dirty and bruised and bumped.

"There were witches and snakes in that shed tonight," wept the goblin, when he was safe at home. "I'll never go there again, never, never, never!"

He never did, so Jack was not scolded any more for dirty tools. They were always clean and bright, hanging neatly in their places. But oh, how they laugh each night when they remember how they punished that rascally goblin! I do wish I'd been there to see it all, don't you?

The Little
Domino House

Bunty was playing in the garden when she heard a funny noise. "Where does that come from?" she wondered. "It sounds as if it's over the wall. I'll go and see."

She peeped over the wall, and at first could see nothing. Then, goodness me, whatever was that in the grass? Surely, surely, it couldn't be an elf!

Bunty felt her cheeks grow red with excitement. Suppose it was! She had always looked for fairies and had never seen one. It really and truly did look like one. And what a funny noise it was making – almost as if it were crying with rage!

Bunty ran to the gate in the wall and opened it. She went to the little figure in the grass and bent down to look at it closely. Yes, sure enough it was an elf, there wasn't a doubt of that. It had a pair of blue wings, and wore a pointed cap and pointed shoes.

It was stamping its feet in the grass, and crying and shouting angrily. When it saw Bunty it shook its tiny fist at her and cried, "Was it you who took my toadstool house away?"

"Goodness, no!" said Bunty. "I've only just this minute come here, because I

heard the noise you were making. What's the matter?"

"Well," said the elf, drying his angry tears on a buttercup petal which he used for a handkerchief, "I grew myself a fine toadstool house, and moved all my furniture in there. The Fairy Queen asked me to send out all the invitations to her next dance, so I told the bumble-bees, who take my messages for me, to come here this evening and fetch the letters. I went out to buy some notepaper, and when I came back my house was gone!"

"Oh dear, I expect someone came along and picked it," said Bunty, feeling very sorry for the little elf. "What are you going to do now? You've nowhere to write, have you?"

"No, and all my furniture is gone too," said the elf sorrowfully. "If only I could grow another toadstool at once it would be all right, but I can't. It takes a whole night to grow one."

Bunty thought for a moment, then she had a wonderful idea.

"Do you know, I think I could build

you a lovely little house," she said. "I could bring my box of dominoes out here and build a house with them. Then I could give you a little chair and table out of my doll's-house, and you could sit down and write all your letters beautifully!"

"Oh, you are good!" cried the elf, in delight. "Do you think you could build the house now?"

Bunty ran off to her bedroom. She took her box of dominoes, a little table and chair, and a cup and saucer from her dolls' tea set, and ran back to the elf. She sat down and found a nice flat piece of grass. Then she began to build a little domino house.

It was rather difficult to build it on the grass, but at last she managed it. It had space left for a window and a nice doorway.

"Could you carry the table and chair in yourself?" Bunty asked the elf. "I'm afraid I might knock the house down if I try to put them in myself."

The elf carried them in, and popped the little cup and saucer on the table. He

was simply delighted with his new house.

"This is lovely!" he said, sitting himself down at the table. "Now, I've got my fountain pen, and here's the paper and envelopes I bought this morning. It won't take me long to write out the invitations. Now I shall be able to have them all ready when the bumble-bees call for them this evening."

Bunty sat down to watch him at work. He wrote very neatly indeed, and it was lovely to watch him sitting at her little doll's-house table, in the domino house she had built. All the morning she watched him, then went in to her lunch. She poured a little lemonade into a thimble and carried it out to the elf. He poured it into his cup and drank it.

"That was good!" he said. "I was dreadfully thirsty. Thank you so much."

All the afternoon and after tea Bunty sat and watched the little elf at work. Then suddenly she heard a loud droning noise, and saw a big crowd of furry bumble-bees flying down. It really was exciting to see them creep into the domino house and go up to the elf's table. He gave them each a letter.

"Take this to Silvertoes," he said to one bee. "Take this to Goldenwings," he said to another. Bunty could have listened all the evening long – but oh, what a pity, her mother called her to come indoors for supper, and off she had to go.

In the morning she ran to the little house – but it wasn't there. The elf had neatly taken it to pieces and stacked all the dominoes inside the box. He had put the table and chair on top of the box, beside the cup and saucer, and covered them all with a dock-leaf in case it rained.

"Well, I suppose that's the last I shall hear of him!" sighed Bunty, as she picked up the things. "What fun it was!"

But it wasn't the last she heard – for what do you think! A big bumble-bee suddenly flew down and dropped a letter

into her lap. Bunty cried out in surprise and opened it.

It was an invitation to the Fairy Queen's dance!

"Please come on full-moon night to the old oak-tree by the pond," said the letter. "There will be dancing and games till cock-crow."

Of course Bunty is going – and wouldn't you love to go with her? I would!

Hot
Potatoes

"You two go and help Daddy today," said Mother. "He's got such a lot to do, sweeping up all the leaves. Take brooms and help him."

"Sweeping is very hard work," said Sam.

"Well, of course, if you are afraid of hard work . . ." began his mother, but Sam stopped her.

"No, Mum, we're not, really we're not! We'll go and help, and we'll sweep hard," he said.

The two of them went out. Their father found some small brooms for them. "You two are mighty good at playing," he said, "now you let me see how good you are at working."

The twins began to sweep hard. There

were such a lot of leaves! The wind was annoying because it would keep blowing them away.

Father made a bonfire of old twigs, plants and rubbish. "Do you want to burn the leaves too?" asked Sam.

"No," said his father. "They go on the compost heap over there. Susie, you go and ask Mummy for some nice small potatoes, will you?"

"What for?" said Susie.

"Well, sweeping up is hungry work," said her father, "and I think we'd all like hot roast potatoes to help us along. Bring me six."

Susie fetched him six. The twins watched him put them in the hot ashes of the bonfire. "Will they cook?" asked Susie. "Will they be nice?"

"Delicious!" said her father. "Now come along, get to work again."

How hard they all worked! By the time four o'clock came they were all very hungry indeed. "I think I'll go and ask Mum for a biscuit," said Sam. But his father called him back.

"No, no. If you're hungry, you can have roast potatoes. There are two for each of us. They'll be done now."

And so they were! Father took them out of the ashes, warm and soft. He and the children ate them standing by the bonfire – and how delicious they were!

"A little reward for hard work!" said Father. "Hot potatoes for all of us!"

The Tale of
Paddy-Paws

Paddy-Paws was a big black cat. He lived
with Miss Sarah and her family at
Number Three, Elm Road, and his
favourite place for sleeping was on the
top of the sunny wall that ran along the
bottom of Miss Sarah's garden.

He was a big cat! His whiskers were
grey and he had a white bib – but all the
rest of him was as black as coal. He was
fat, lazy and sleepy, and Miss Sarah's
cook said he wasn't a bit of good to
anybody.

"He just eats and sleeps, sleeps and
eats!" she said. "Miss Sarah spoils him. If
Paddy-Paws were mine I'd spank him!"

Now one day Cook found that there
had been mice in her larder. They had
nibbled at the cheese, eaten the bread,

and upset the milk. She was very cross!

"Hey, Paddy-Paws!" she cried. "Come here! There have been mice in my larder. Mice, I said! You don't look a bit excited as a good cat should! You ought to be ashamed of yourself, so you ought, to let a mouse come into the house where you live! It shows how little they care for you! They don't take the slightest bit of notice of a lazy cat like you! You should be out chasing them away!"

Paddy-Paws felt most annoyed. What, expect a grand cat like him to catch mice?

Whatever could Cook be thinking of? He wasn't brought up to catch mice like any common cat!

Paddy-Paws sat on the wall that morning and sunned himself. He didn't know that Cook had gone into the dining-room to tell Miss Sarah about the mice in the larder.

"Miss Sarah," said Cook, "whatever do you think? Those horrid mice have been in the larder!"

"Mice!" cried Miss Sarah, her face turning quite pale. "Good gracious me! If there's one thing I'm really frightened of, it's a mouse!"

"Oh, I'm not frightened of them, silly little creatures," said Cook. "They're harmless enough – but once they are in the larder, it's hard to get rid of them!"

"But why doesn't Paddy-Paws catch them?" asked Miss Sarah.

"I'll tell you why he doesn't, Miss Sarah," said Cook, "it's because he's too well fed and too lazy! That's why! What cat is going to catch mice if he gets three good meals a day, I should like to know?

He's so fat he can hardly swing his tail!"

"Dear me!" said Miss Sarah. "Is that so? Well, Cook, perhaps he should only be fed once a day. Tell him that until he catches the mice in the larder he must miss two meals a day."

"Oh, he'll catch mice soon enough if we let him go hungry," said Cook. "Thank you, Miss Sarah."

Out she went into the kitchen. It was time to put down a dish of fish and milk for Paddy-Paws, but Cook smiled to herself and gave it to the dog next door. Paddy-Paws was surprised to find his bowl empty when he came in to eat his lunch.

"Listen, Paddy-Paws," said Cook, sternly. "There are mice to be caught – *mice*! Do you hear me? Well, Miss Sarah says until you do your duty and catch those mice you are only to have one meal

a day. So be sensible and work for your living like any other cat!"

Well! Paddy-Paws couldn't believe his ears! So that was how they were going to treat him, was it? He wasn't going to stay here a minute longer then. No, he would go straight off and find another home where he would be properly treated.

And off he went! Out of the front gate, his tail up in the air. He walked for a long way and then came to a nice little house that smelled of frying fish.

Paddy-Paws sniffed hungrily. He would go and live here! He walked up to the kitchen door and mewed loudly. A lady was in the kitchen, cooking lunch for her two children.

"Donald! Peggy! Here is a beautiful cat!" she called. "Come and see him!"

Paddy-Paws was pleased. He let the children pick him up and take him indoors.

"Let's dress him up in your doll's clothes," said Donald. Then, to Paddy-Paws' great horror, they put a petticoat on him, then a dress, and then a bonnet! He

struggled and mewed, but the children wouldn't let him go.

"Look, Mother, look!" they cried – but Paddy-Paws shook all the clothes off himself in a rage and tore out of the door. He wasn't going to live there! Miss Sarah had never made him wear silly clothes like that!

Out into the road he went and wandered on until he came to a pretty farmhouse. He went to the kitchen door and looked in. The farmer and his family were sitting round the table, eating.

"Look, Dad, look!" cried one of the children. "See that fine big cat looking in at the door. I guess he's big enough to kill all those rats we've got in the barn!"

"Come here, Puss!" said the farmer. He picked up the cat and took him across the farmyard to the barn.

"Here you are," he said, opening a door. "Get in there and kill a few rats for me. Then you shall have a saucer of cream!"

He shut Paddy-Paws in and the cat looked round in rage. How dare the farmer shut him into a horrid barn to catch rats. What were rats, anyway? He had never seen one in his life!

Suddenly a lean, grey creature ran out of a corner and looked at him.

"Pooh, a cowardly cat!" it said, and began to nibble at a sack of grain. Then another rat came out and yet another until the barn was full of them. Paddy-Paws felt afraid. Suppose they all ran at him and bit him? Whatever would he do?

After a while the farmer opened the door and looked in. He saw Paddy-Paws sitting quietly in the middle of the floor with all the rats feasting round him! How angry he was!

"Do you call yourself a cat?" he roared. "Why, a kitten would do better!"

He went to give Paddy-Paws a cuff on the back, and the surprised cat fled away. He began to wish he had never left his own comfortable home.

He went on again until he came to a beautiful house. He slipped indoors and found himself in a room with a warm fire. A pretty lady was sitting reading.

"Why, Puss!" she said. "What a beauty you are! I wish you were my cat!"

Paddy-Paws was pleased. He thought he would live in this house. He sat down by the pretty lady and purred. Yes, he would live here.

Suddenly the door opened and in came two terrier dogs! They frisked all over the place, and then they saw Paddy-Paws.

"Wuff! Wuff! Wuff!" they cried, and after him they went. What a shock he got! He rushed out of the door and jumped up a tree in the garden, the larger dog just managing to nip a few hairs out

of his tail as he jumped.

"My goodness me!" cried Paddy-Paws, "I couldn't live there! Fancy having two rough dogs like that! Miss Sarah has never kept dogs. Oh, how I wish I was back at home – but I'm afraid that now I've run away they won't want me back!"

Paddy-Paws didn't dare to get down the tree as long as there was daylight in case the dogs chased him again. So there he had to stay until it was dark – then, hungry and tired, he trotted back to Number Three, where his mistress, Miss Sarah, lived.

He slipped in at the back door. Cook was out. The kitchen was dark. There was nothing in Paddy-Paws' dish in the corner. Poor Paddy-Paws! He was very hungry.

Suddenly he heard a noise in the larder – mice! Paddy-Paws crept to the door and looked in. The mice at once ran away. Paddy-Paws felt excited. He thought he would like a meal of mice, because he was so very hungry. So he slipped inside the door and waited in the darkness.

And will you believe it, when Cook came in and went to the larder, there sat Paddy-Paws with six dead mice around him!

"Did you ever see anything like it!" cried Cook, and ran straight to Miss Sarah to tell her – and oh, what a lot of petting Paddy-Paws had then! He was patted and stroked, and given a saucer of bread and milk for a reward. He was so hungry that he ate it all up straightaway.

"What did I tell you!" said Cook. "Let

113

him go a bit short on his meals and he'll catch mice as well as any other cat!"

"Mew, mew, mew. I only caught those mice because I've had some horrid adventures today and I was glad to be home again!" said Paddy-Paws. "But I've learned my lesson. There's no place like home – and I'll do my duty now, and keep the house free from mice. Pur-rrr-rrr!"

And ever since then there hasn't been a single mouse at Number Three!

The Higgledy Piggledy Goblins

Once upon a time there were two bad goblins. One was called Higgledy – he was the tall, thin one – and the other was called Piggledy. He was short and fat. But they were both horrid little creatures, and nobody liked them a bit.

They were very clever. They knew a good many spells which they had stolen from wizards on their travels, and they would use these spells if the people they met would not give them what they wanted.

It wasn't very nice to be turned into a jumpity frog. It was even nastier to be blown down a rabbit-hole and kept prisoner there for a week or two while Higgledy and Piggledy took what they wanted. That was the sort of thing the two goblins did, so it was no wonder that nobody liked them at all.

The goblins had gone travelling through the villages of Pixieland. They had demanded gold wherever they went, and were carrying a large sack of gold pieces between them. They meant to go back to their goblin-cave as rich as could be, and never do any more work for the rest of their lives.

Nobody in Pixieland liked to refuse them when they demanded gold. They would come stalking into a peaceful pixie village, sound their long trumpet, call the people round them and tell them that unless they gave them ten gold pieces by the next morning, somebody would be punished. And as that somebody was usually the head pixie, he soon collected ten gold pieces and gave them to the goblins. Then, the next day, they would shoulder their heavy sack again and march off to the next village.

Now there was a small village called Twittering in the heart of Pixieland, and the head pixie, Chinks, was clever. He felt sure that sooner or later the goblins would come to Twittering and he made up his mind to trick them. His village was poor and he was not going to make his people pay ten gold pieces to the robber goblins.

One day, sure enough, the two goblins appeared, staggering under their sack,

which was now very heavy indeed – almost full, in fact! They stood in the middle of Twittering, and Higgledy blew his trumpet. At once a crowd gathered round and Piggledy spoke loudly.

"Where is the head pixie?"

"Here," said Chinks, stepping forward.

"Get us ten gold pieces from the people of your village before morning – or you will be sorry!" said Piggledy.

"And find us somewhere soft and warm to sleep," commanded Higgledy.

"Come to a little house I have for my friends," said Chinks at once. He led the way and the two goblins followed. They soon came to a small toadstool house, neat and cosy, with just enough room in it for two people.

Next door to it was a farm shed, and from this shed there came a curious gobbling noise.

"What's that?" asked the goblins, in surprise.

"Oh, those are goblin-gobblers," said Chinks. "But you needn't be afraid – they are tightly shut in."

The goblins had never heard of goblin-gobblers before, and they looked rather scared.

"What are they like?" said Higgledy.

"I'll show you," said Chinks, going towards the door of the shed as if he meant to open it.

"No, no!" shouted the goblins, at once. "We don't want to see. What a strange noise they make. What are they saying?"

"Oh, they just say, 'We gobble goblins, we gobble goblins,'" said Chinks. "Can't you hear them?"

The goblins listened. Yes, certainly, the noise did sound like those words. How horrid!

"Are you sure they are safely shut in?" asked the goblins, nervously.

"Oh quite," said Chinks. "Now if you like to go into your house, goblins, I will have supper sent in to you, and later on at night I will come with the gold pieces I have collected. It will take me a little time to get them all."

The goblins scurried into their toadstool house and bolted the door. They wished they were not so near the goblin-gobblers, but it couldn't be helped. They would be safe with their door shut.

Soon a good supper was sent to them, and they unbolted their door and took it in. They ate it all and waited for Chinks to come. He was very late indeed. It was almost midnight when they heard him knocking at the door.

"You are late," said Higgledy.

"I know," said Chinks, "but we are poor and ten gold pieces needed a lot of collecting."

The goblins opened their sack and Chinks came forward with his gold. As he was counting it into the sack there came a terrible noise outside.

"Gobble-gobble-gobble-gobble!"

"My goodness!" shouted Chinks. "The goblin-gobblers have got loose! Run for your lives, goblins! They will gobble you up!"

"Gobble-gobble-gobble-gobble!" came the noise, nearer and nearer. The goblins fled out of the door into the night, scared out of their wits. They saw, in the dim moonlight, a crowd of strange, noisy shapes, crying "Gobble-gobble-gobble-gobble!"

With a shriek they tore away as fast as their legs could carry them, and didn't stop until they had safely returned to Goblinland. And so scared were they of meeting goblin-gobblers after that, that they never once left Goblinland again!

As soon as they had gone, Chinks chuckled and lit a lantern. He swung its light on to the gobblers.

"Come, turkeys, come, turkeys, back to bed!" he cried. "You have done your part well!"

"Gobble-gobble-gobble-gobble," said all the turkeys, following Chinks back to the barn. He shut them in and went back to the toadstool house. He lay down on the bed, after carefully bolting the door, and went to sleep.

In the morning he called all the people of Twittering to him and told them how he had scared the bad goblins with his flock of turkeys – and how those pixies laughed and chuckled!

"And here," said Chinks, pulling the heavy sack before him, "is all the gold that the goblins have taken from the little villages throughout Pixieland. First we will take from it our own ten gold pieces, and then we will send the others back to where they came from."

He was as good as his word, and the pixie villages were delighted to receive back all the gold they had so unwillingly given to the two goblins. The fame of Chinks's clever trick went far and wide – and very soon he was made King of all Pixieland!

"Three cheers for clever old Chinks!" cried everyone. "And three cheers for his good old goblin-gobblers!"

And Chinks's turkeys, who had come to see their master crowned king, waved their long necks in delight, and cried at the tops of their voices:

"Gobble-gobble-gobble-gobble!"

Cross
Aunt Tabitha

Aunt Tabitha was rather a strict old lady.
When her nieces went to stay with her,
they were very careful how they behaved.
They said "please" and "thank you" when
they should, and they always opened the
door for Aunt Tabitha and fetched her
footstool as soon as she sat in her chair.

When Sally and Jane went to stay with
her they felt rather frightened. They did
hope they would do everything they
should. They meant to try very hard.

But Sally was rather a noisy child and
banged doors behind her. So Aunt Tabitha
was cross and spoke sharply.

And then Jane upset her tea all over
the clean tablecloth and that made Aunt
Tabitha cross too. They went to bed the
first night feeling rather upset.

"I hope Aunt Tabitha isn't going to be cross all the time," said Sally.

"I shall go home if she is!" said Jane. "I don't like her."

"Well, we'll see what happens to-morrow," said Sally. "I shall try my hardest not to bang doors."

She didn't bang a door – but she forgot to wipe her feet on the mat and brought mud in all over the blue hall carpet. Aunt Tabitha frowned when she saw it.

"Get the vacuum cleaner and clear up the mud as soon as it is dry," she said.

And then Jane knocked against a little table, upset a glass vase and down it went with a crash. It broke into about a hundred pieces!

Aunt Tabitha was very angry. "If you are clumsy again I shall send you up to bed," she said.

Poor Sally and Jane! It was really very difficult for them to be sweet and smiling to someone who scolded them so hard. But they knew that Aunt Tabitha was old, and Mother had said that old people were not so patient as younger ones.

"She's nice when she smiles," said Sally. "But I wish she'd smile more often."

"I think we'll go home," said Jane, who was rather afraid of being sent to bed if she did anything else to displease her aunt. "I'll pack our bag. We can slip out of the house and go home without anyone knowing."

Just then Aunt Tabitha's daily help came in, looking very pale. "Please, Sally and Jane," she said. "I don't feel well. Do you think you could manage to get your aunt's tea if I leave it ready?"

"Of course," said Jane at once. "Go home, Mary. You do look ill. We can manage."

"I meant to finish turning out your aunt's little sewing-room," said Mary. "I'm in the middle of it now. But I feel so ill I really think I'd better leave it until tomorrow."

Mary went home. The two girls looked at one another. "We can't slip home now," said Jane. "It would be mean. We must stay and help."

"Do you think we'd better try and finish turning out Aunt Tabitha's sewing-room?" said Sally. "It would be kind to Mary to do it. And Aunt Tabitha does hate to see a room upside down. Let's do it!"

So the two girls got dusters, polish, brushes and the vacuum cleaner, and went to finish turning out the sewing-room. Aunt Tabitha was having a nap in the living-room, and didn't know what they were doing at all.

The room was upside down, for Mary had been right in the middle of turning it

out. The girls swept the ceiling free of cobwebs. They hoovered the carpet. They polished the furniture. Then they wondered if they ought to take the chair cushions into the garden and bang them to get rid of the dust.

"Well, we might as well be thorough!" said Jane. "Look – the seat of this chair comes out. Shall we take it right out and clean underneath properly?"

"Yes," said Sally. "Come on – tug!"

The seat of the chair, which was an enormous velvet cushion, came out with a jerk. The girls were just going to take it downstairs to shake it when Jane caught sight of something deep down in the underseat of the chair. She put her hand down and pulled it out. It was a flat leather case. She opened it – and gave a loud cry.

"Sally! This notecase is full of money.

Look – five and ten pound notes! Good gracious! Who do you suppose it belongs to?"

"I can't imagine. We'll tell Aunt Tabitha at teatime and see what she says," said Sally, excited. "I daren't wake her now. Come on – let's finish our job. Put the case somewhere safe until tea-time."

At teatime the two girls took in the tea tray most carefully. Sally had made the tea, and had filled the hot-water jug. The bread-and-butter was already cut. The cake Jane had taken out of the tin and put on a plate.

"Dear me! Where is Mary?" asked Aunt Tabitha in surprise, when the girls came in with the tea things.

"She's not feeling well," said Jane. "So she went home. She was in the middle of turning out your little sewing-room, Aunt Tabitha, and we thought we would finish it for her. We took the big seat out of the old armchair there, to shake the dust from it – and right down under the seat we found this!"

131

Jane gave her aunt the leather case. Aunt Tabitha stared at it in the greatest amazement and delight.

"My lost notecase!" she cried. "Oh, to think it's found again! There was eighty pounds in it! I lost it nearly two years ago, and hunted for it everywhere! Well, well, well!"

"Oh, Aunt Tabitha – I am pleased for you!" cried Sally. "I know how horrid it is to lose things – and how lovely to find them again!"

"I do think you are good children to finish turning out the sewing-room," said Aunt Tabitha. "And to think you were thorough enough to take the cushion-seat out of the chair to shake! Well, well! I've thought you were rather careless children – but I'm sorry I thought that now. I think you are good and helpful children, and I am pleased with you !"

Sally and Jane went red with pleasure. They each thought how nearly they had slipped away and gone home, but they did not want to tell Aunt Tabitha that. Instead they sat and ate a good tea, and had two slices of cake each because Aunt Tabitha was so pleased with them.

And the next day their aunt asked Mary to take them shopping. She bought a big baby-doll for Jane, with eyes that opened and shut, and a book for Sally.

"That's your share of the eighty pounds you found!" said Aunt Tabitha, when they came back and thanked her. "Nice children! Good children! I'm glad you are staying with me!"

"We're glad, too," said Jane, and she

hugged her aunt hard. And, dear me, wasn't it a good thing they didn't run away the day before! You never know how things are going to turn out, do you? It's always best to go on trying, no matter what happens.

Dame Crabby's
Surprise Packet

Dame Crabby lived on the outside of Tipkin Village, and the little folk who lived there were very glad that she didn't live right in the village itself. She was a cross old dame, and as lazy as could be. Her cottage was dark and dirty, and spiders simply loved to weave their cobwebs in every corner.

Tipkin Village was a very spick and span place. The steps to each cottage were as white as snow, the little gardens were full of bright flowers, and the curtains at each window were always clean.

Tipkin Village was trying to win the prize that the King of Fairyland gave each year for the best-kept village. Jinkie the gnome and Popple the pixie went round every day to remind all the little folk to weed their gardens, keep their chimneys swept, wash their curtains, whiten their front steps and shine up their door-knockers.

But, of course, nobody could do anything with old Dame Crabby. She just simply would not do what she was told. She kept her steps disgracefully – they were really black with dirt. As for her windows, you couldn't even see through them to know if her curtains were clean or not. Her garden was a mass of weeds, her chimney smoked, there wasn't a clean

spot in the whole of her cottage, and Dame Crabby herself looked like a bundle of old clothes.

"She'll prevent us from winning the prize," groaned Jinkie and Popple. "It's a shame. Dame Crabby, it is mean of you. Won't you at least try to be clean and tidy?"

The funny thing was that Dame Crabby didn't seem to see that her cottage was dirty!

"What's the matter with it?" she would ask. "Didn't I sweep up the floor this very morning? And didn't I pull up a thistle yesterday?"

"Oh dear, that's not nearly enough to keep a house and garden tidy and neat!" sighed Jinkie. "Look here, Dame Crabby, will you go out for the day, to visit your cousin Sarah? Then we'll all come in and make your cottage and your garden simply beautiful."

"Well, I don't mind doing that," said Dame Crabby. So it was arranged that she should go the next day and catch the half-past eight bus.

But of course she overslept and missed the bus and then she wouldn't go. The little folk were almost in tears about it.

"I can't think what you are worrying about," said Dame Crabby, crossly. "Anyone would think my cottage was dirty to hear you talk. I really can't see anything the matter with it and I never shall. Do go away and leave me in peace."

The little folk went away sadly. They had brought brooms and dusters, scrubbing-brushes and mops, meaning to have a good clean-up if only Dame Crabby had gone to visit her cousin. But it was no use now.

"I'll go and ask Mister Tubby, the wise man in the next village, if he can help us," said Jinkie at last. "He may have a good idea."

So off he went. He told Mister Tubby his trouble, and the little, fat, wise man listened. He sat and thought for a long time, and then he got up from his chair and took a little blue box from a cupboard.

"I'll send her a spot of sunshine," he

138

said. "Sometimes a spot of sunshine will show people how dusty and dirty things are, when nothing else will. I'll pack it into this pretty box in the form of a golden star that shines brightly. Dame Crabby will wear it as a brooch. It will be a great surprise for her!"

He drew a circle round a ray of sunshine that lay on the table. He muttered a few magic words, and when the sun went behind a cloud, and the sunshine fled, a little spot still lay on the table, winking and blinking away brightly

in the circle of chalk. It was like a little golden star, very beautiful to see.

Carefully Mister Tubby picked it up and slipped it inside the blue box. He tied it round with string and gave it to Jinkie, who was very grateful.

"Post it on your way home," said the wise man. Jinkie thanked him and said goodbye. He stopped at the post office and posted it to Dame Crabby. Then he went home to Tipkin Village to tell all the little folk there what he had done.

Next morning the blue box arrived at Dame Crabby's. How surprised she was, for she never got parcels or letters! She opened the box and had an even greater surprise – for the sunshine star shone out so brightly that it dazzled her eyes!

"Goodness me!" she cried. "What a lovely thing! It's a brooch, the finest ever I saw! Now who in the world has sent me that?"

She put it on the front of her dress where it shone like a little lamp. How pleased the old dame was! She took up her knitting and sang a little song to

herself, she was so happy. Then she dropped her ball of wool, and down on the floor she went to look for it.

The spot of sunshine shone into the dark corners there, and my, how dirty they were! Dame Crabby was shocked.

"Bless us!" she cried. "I'd no idea the floor was so dirty! I must scrub it!"

So she scrubbed it till it shone as white as snow. Then she went to the larder to get herself a bit of bread and cheese –

141

and the sunshine star shone brightly into that dark cupboard, showing up grey cobwebs in the corners, stale spots of grease on the dirty shelves, and crumbs all over the place.

Dame Crabby stared in surprise.

"Well, who would have thought my larder was so dirty!" she cried. "Just look at that! I must certainly clean it today!"

So she set to work and cleaned it out. It took quite a time, for it was really

dreadfully dirty. It looked beautiful when she had finished. The sunshine star shone round it and the shelves gleamed white and the cobwebs were all gone. Dame Crabby was pleased.

When she went to bed that night she put the spot of sunshine on the chest beside her. It shone on to the bedclothes and she saw that they wanted washing. It shone on to her dress over the bed-rail and she saw that it wanted mending. It shone on to her washstand and dear me, how cracked and old the basin and jug looked!

"I must do some shopping," said Dame Crabby, before she fell asleep. "I want some nice new things. Ho, ho! Those folk down in Tipkin Village wanted to come and clean out my cottage, did they, and make it as spotless as theirs? Well, I'll show them a thing or two! I'm richer than any of them, and I'll go and buy the prettiest curtains in the kingdom and a fine new dress of red silk for myself, and a new basin and a jug of blue china, and – and – and . . ."

But by that time she was fast asleep.

Dame Crabby put on her sunshine brooch next day, and once again it lit up the dirty corners. In the morning she cleaned and scrubbed, and in the afternoon she went shopping. My, the things she bought!

She was so pleased with herself in her dress of red silk that she thought she would give a party. But first she went poking and prying into all the dark corners of her cottage, the sunshine star lighting up every cobweb, every bit of dirt and every speck of dust. It was marvellous, really! Dame Crabby was so pleased with herself for finding the dirty corners; she didn't for one moment think it was the sunshine brooch she wore!

All the little folk of the village were watching and waiting to see what would happen – and how delighted they were to see that the spot of sunshine was doing its work!

"If only Dame Crabby would see what a mess her garden is in, everything would be all right!" they said.

Well, that very morning Dame Crabby took a chair into the garden to have a rest, for she felt a little tired. And her sunshine brooch shone into the tangled weeds and lit up a lovely red rose, almost choked by nettles and thistles!

Dame Crabby saw the rose glowing there.

"Dear dear!" she said, "look at that wonderful rose trying to bloom in that mess of weeds. I must pull them up so that it can bloom properly. It's a very lovely rose."

Then the spot of sunshine fell on a patch of sweet williams, trying in vain to poke their bright heads above the weeds. Dame Crabby saw them too, and up she jumped. She began to weed! My, what a lot she pulled up! Then she thought she would cut her grass and weed the path, too.

By the time she was ready to give her party her cottage and her garden were just as fine as anyone else's. She sent out her invitations, asked Matty Mouse to come and help her hand round the cakes and pour out the tea, and put on her fine new dress of red silk.

All the folk of Tipkin Village came to her party – and how they praised her new curtains, her new carpet, and her lovely new eiderdown! Nobody said anything at all about the spot of sunshine gleaming on Dame Crabby's dress, but they all chuckled to themselves to think how that little speck of sunlight had made such a change in the old dame's cottage!

Just as they were sitting down to tea, there came the sound of galloping horses

– and who should arrive in Tipkin Village that sunny afternoon but the King of Fairyland himself, come to see if the village was well kept enough to win the prize. He was so surprised when he found everyone out – but he had a good look at all the empty houses and was delighted to see them so pretty and neat.

Then he drove to the only house in the village that had smoke coming from its chimney, and that was Dame Crabby's – and in at the front door he walked and sat down with all the astonished and delighted folk to have a cup of tea and a slice of Matty Mouse's brown ginger-

bread. Goodness, what an excitement there was!

Well, of course, Tipkin Village got the prize, and it was a big sack of gold.

"We must take ten pieces of it to Mister Tubby, the wise man!" cried Jinkie and Popple.

"But why?" asked Dame Crabby in surprise. "He hasn't had anything to do with our winning the prize!"

"Oh yes, he has!" cried Jinkie, pointing to the sunshine brooch gleaming on the old dame's dress. "We got that from him – and it made you clean up your cottage and make your garden as nice as anyone else's!"

Well, at first Dame Crabby frowned to think of the trick that had been played on her – but when she looked round and saw her pretty new curtains, her nice silk dress and all the laughing folk of Tipkin Village eating her lovely tea, she was glad and she laughed, too. She took off the sunshine star and gave it to Jinkie.

"I shan't need it any more," she said. "Give it to someone else!"

So Jinkie keeps it to send to people who are not as clean and tidy as they should be. I don't want it to be sent to me, but I'd love to see it, wouldn't you?

The Goblin Who Broke
His Glasses

John and Dora were very sad. It was their mother's birthday the very next day, and they had lost the money that they had saved up for seven weeks. They had meant to buy their mother a lovely bottle of perfume, and now they could buy her nothing.

"It is bad luck!" said John. "I had the money in my pocket, and I thought it was quite safe there. I didn't know there was a hole at the bottom. The money must have dropped out yesterday when we ran down that grassy hill."

"What are we to do?" asked Dora. "We really must buy Mummy something. It would be dreadful if she didn't have a present from us."

"Yes, I know," said John. "But I don't

see what we can do, Dora. We can't very well ask Mum for some money to buy her own birthday present with – and Daddy's gone to town."

"Well, we'd better go to the hill we ran down yesterday and try to find our money," said Dora. "That's the only thing I can think of!"

So they put on their jackets and went. They soon got to the hill, but although they looked simply everywhere they could see no sign of their lost money at all. They were very disappointed.

"We'd better go home," said John, with a sigh. "We'll tell Mum, then she won't expect a present. We'll tell her that we'll save up again, and give her a present as soon as we can. She knows I lost some money through that hole so perhaps she won't mind her present being late."

So they turned to go back home again. But just as they got halfway down the hill, Dora stopped and clutched John's arm.

"Look, John!" she said in a whisper. "What's that over there, sitting on that stile? It isn't a boy and it isn't a man."

John looked, and then he rubbed his eyes in astonishment. He looked again – but it was quite true; there was a small goblin dressed in green and red, sitting on the stile!

"Why, it's a goblin!" said John. "It really is! But Dora, how exciting! We've never seen any of the fairy-folk in our lives before, and here is a real, live goblin sitting on a stile!"

The two children stared at the little creature for some time. He didn't move, and he didn't seem to see them. He just sat there quite still.

"Let's go and speak to him," said Dora, feeling very bold.

So they walked down the hill to where the stile led into a corn-field. The goblin heard them coming, and he raised his big pointed ears and listened – but still he didn't seem to see them.

"Hello, Goblin!" said John. "I say, are you really a goblin?"

"Of course," said the goblin. "What are you? Children, by the sound of you!"

"Yes, we're children, a girl and a boy," said John. "But can't you see us?"

"No," said the goblin, and he blinked his eyes. "I've broken my glasses. I can't see a thing without them. That's why I'm sitting here. I tripped over a stone and fell. My glasses shot off my nose and were smashed to pieces. So I thought if I waited here long enough I should find someone kind enough to lead me safely home. I've another pair of glasses there, you see."

"Well, shall we take you home?" asked Dora, kindly. "You could tell us the way to go, couldn't you?"

"Oh, yes," said the goblin, jumping off the stile. "Would you pick up the frame of my glasses, please? Thank you, little girl. I can get some new lenses put into them, and then I shall have two pairs again. Now, would you each take one of my hands, and lead me carefully home. I will tell you the way."

So they each took one of the goblin's hands and started off.

"Go across the field, and halfway to the next stile you will see a very big

oak-tree," said the goblin. "Stop just by it, please."

They took him halfway across the field and stopped by an old oak. The goblin put out his hands and felt all round the trunk. He pressed a knob of bark, and suddenly the whole side of the tree disappeared, and the surprised children saw a stairway inside, leading downwards. They all stepped into the tree, and the trunk closed up again.

There was a lamp hanging above, so John and Dora could see their way down. They took the goblin's hands again, and carefully led him downwards.

"When you come to the bottom, you will see three doors," said the goblin. "Open the middle one, and go down the passage beyond. You will soon come to some toadstools. Choose three red ones side by side, and we will sit upon them."

It was just as the goblin said. At the end of the stairway were three doors, one painted yellow, one red and one green. The middle one was yellow, and the children opened it. Beyond was a narrow,

winding passage. They all went down it, and came to a large cave in which toadstools of every colour grew. They were very large, and John looked all about for three red ones side by side. He found them at last, and led the goblin towards them.

The three sat down on the toadstools, and the goblin muttered some magic words. Suddenly they all shot upwards at a terrific pace, and John and Dora gasped for breath. Up and up went the toadstools, and then came to a stop out in the open air.

"Here we are," said the gnome. "Now, if you'll kindly take my hands again, and lead me to the fifth cottage in the row by the beech tree, that's the end of our journey."

John and Dora saw a higgledy-piggledy row of funny little cottages in the shade of a large beech tree. They led the goblin to the fifth one, which was called Ho-Ho Cottage, and the little man took out a key. He unlocked the front door, and went inside. When he came out he was wearing a very large pair of round glasses.

"That's better!" he said. "Now I can see properly! It's dreadful not to be able to see anything. Will you please come in and have some chocolate cake and a glass of lemonade?"

The children were delighted. They went inside Ho-Ho Cottage and sat down. It was the tiniest little place. The goblin brought out a very large chocolate cake and a jug of home-made lemonade. John and Dora were soon munching hungrily.

"Wasn't it lucky for you we were on the hill?" said Dora. "You might have

waited all day before anyone passed, because very few people go that way."

"What were you doing there?" asked the goblin. John told him all about the lost money, and how sorry they were not to be able to buy anything for their mother's birthday.

"Dear, dear, that's very sad," said the goblin. "But wait now! I have an idea! I could show you where some very fine mushrooms grow. You could pick them, and then sell them at the market, couldn't you? The money you get for them would buy your mother a fine present! Would you like that?"

"Ooh, yes!" said both the children together.

So when they had finished their cake and lemonade, the goblin took them outside.

"Wait a minute!" he said. "You haven't got a basket with you. I'll lend you my biggest one, but would you mind letting me have it back? You could leave it outside that old oak-tree in the field for me."

"Yes, we will," said John. The goblin fetched a big basket, and they all set off together. They went back the way they had come, and when they had reached the cornfield, the goblin took them to a green meadow not very far away. And there, near to a ditch, was the finest crop of mushrooms the children had ever seen!

"I'll leave you now if you don't mind," said the goblin. "I've got to go and see my tailor about a new coat. Good luck to you, and mind you pick all the mushrooms you want! Thank you for being kind to me."

"Goodbye, and thank you too!" cried

the children. "Don't forget to get your glasses mended!"

The goblin vanished. The two children set to work picking the mushrooms. It was not long before they had the gnome's big basket full to the brim.

"Now we'll go to the market," said John. "We'll carry the basket between us. Isn't it heavy, Dora?"

When they got to the market, they went to a farmer's wife they knew, who had a stall with greens, butter and pots of cream spread out on it. She cried out in surprise when she saw the mushrooms.

"Lawksamussy me, where did you get those wonderful mushrooms?" she cried. "You sell them to me before anyone else sees them! I'll give you a good price for them!"

The children were glad to empty the basket into her box. She weighed the mushrooms, and then said she would give them three pounds for the lot.

"Oh, that's lovely!" cried John. "Fifty pence more than we had before! Oh, thank you, Mrs Mooly."

The farmer's wife paid them, and they ran off to the shop that sold perfume. They bought a lovely bottle of cologne, and then turned to go home, for it was getting near their dinner-time. They took the goblin's basket with them, and when they came to the oak-tree they left it outside as the goblin had asked them.

Their mother was so pleased with her birthday present next day.

"My favourite perfume!" she cried. "Oh, you kind children! But, my dears, how did you manage to buy it? I thought you had lost your money."

Then the children told her about the little goblin, and she could hardly believe her ears.

"We'll go this very morning to that old oak-tree and try to find the stairway inside!" she said.

So off they went. The basket was gone, of course, for the goblin had fetched it the night before. The children tried hard to find the knob of bark that would make the side of the tree disappear, but they couldn't. Wasn't it a pity?

"We'll find it one day!" cried John. "And then, well, hurrah for another exciting adventure!"

The Left-Behind
Bunny

Jimmy had a beautiful toy bunny that
he loved very much and always took to
bed with him. It was white all over, and
had pink eyes and pink insides to its ears.
Its name was Bobtail, and it really was a
lovely rabbit.

One day Jimmy took it to his Auntie
Susan's to tea. His aunt had a fine tea –
chocolate cake, jam sandwich and
bananas and cream. Jimmy enjoyed it
very much, and he got himself covered
with chocolate, jam and cream.

"Good gracious, Jimmy!" said his
mother. "You are covered with bits of
your tea. May he go to the bathroom and
wash himself, Auntie Susan?"

"Certainly," said his aunt, so off went
Jimmy. He took his bunny with him, and

sat him on the bathroom stool whilst he washed his hands. It took him a long time, because they were really very sticky indeed. He was so long that his mother called up the stairs to him.

"Jimmy! Whatever are you doing? Do hurry up, because Auntie wants you to go and see if the hens have laid any eggs."

Now if there was one thing that Jimmy really did love, it was going to look for eggs. He dried his hands and rushed downstairs – and he quite forgot about poor old Bobtail, sitting on the stool.

He went to look for the eggs and found seven. Then it was time to go home, and his mother and Jimmy had to run for the bus – and when they were inside and safely on the way home, Jimmy remembered his rabbit.

"Oh, Mummy, stop the bus and go back!" he cried. "I've left Bobtail behind."

"Well, you must go and get him tomorrow," said his mother. "It's too late to go back now."

"But he'll be so lonely and cold sitting up on the bathroom stool all night by himself," said Jimmy, with tears in his eyes. "And besides, Mummy, I couldn't go to bed without him, I really couldn't. I'd be so lonely myself."

"Well, darling, we can't go back to Auntie's," said his mother. "Now don't be silly. We shall soon be home, and you'll be in bed and asleep before you know what's what. Then in the morning you can fetch Bobtail."

But Jimmy wouldn't be comforted. He kept thinking of the bunny sitting on the stool, waiting to be fetched, and feeling all alone and forgotten. He cried all the way home, he cried going to bed, and he cried when he was in bed. It was really dreadful.

His mother got cross with him at last, and turned out the light and left him. Jimmy still wept all by himself, for he missed Bobtail terribly, and felt very mean to have forgotten his dear old rabbit.

The toys in the toy cupboard heard him crying. They knew quite well what he was sad about, for they had heard him begging his mother to send someone to fetch Bobtail from his auntie's. They all loved Jimmy, and couldn't bear to hear him crying in his bed.

"Can't we do something?" whispered the sailor-doll.

"If only we could get Bobtail for him he would be happy again," said the teddy bear. "But how can we? It is much too far for us to walk, and the toy motor-car is broken."

"What about Jimmy's new aeroplane?" asked the elephant. "Couldn't we fly off in that, and fetch Bobtail?"

All the toys thought that was a splendid idea. The bear thought he could fly the aeroplane, if it would promise not to come down till he told it to, and the sailor-doll said he would go with him for company. So they quietly wheeled the tiny aeroplane on to the bedroom floor, got into it, and flew out of the window.

They did feel excited! They flew down the road and then over the fields to Jimmy's aunt's house. Then they landed on the bathroom windowsill and peeped into the room. Sure enough, there was poor old Bobtail bunny, all by himself on the bathroom stool!

"Hi, Bobtail!" called the sailor-doll, softly. "Come on! We've come to fetch you! We've got the aeroplane here!"

The bunny jumped off the stool and hurried to the window. He had tears in both his eyes, but he soon wiped them away, and laughed for joy to see his friends there, waiting for him. In a minute he was in the aeroplane too, and it rose into the air once more.

It was not long before it was back on the bedroom floor, and the bear, the sailor-doll and the bunny climbed out.

"Thank you ever so much!" whispered the bunny, and ran straight to Jimmy's bed. He jumped up, and snuggled down beside the little boy.

"Ooh!" cried Jimmy in delight. "Ooh! It's my bunny again! Oh, Bobtail, I am

so very glad to see you again!"

He fell asleep smiling, and in the morning he thanked his mother for sending someone to fetch his bunny for him.

"But I didn't!" said his mother, and she did look surprised to see Bobtail there. She simply couldn't understand how the bunny had come back, and neither could Jimmy. But the toys could have told them, couldn't they?

171

On Christmas Night

"Now you twins must go to sleep quickly or Santa Claus won't come and fill your stockings," said Mother, on Christmas Eve.

The twins talked after she had gone. "I always try to stay awake but I never can," said Dan. "I wish we could wake up when Santa Claus comes upstairs."

"I know what we'll do!" said Daisy. "We'll put a box by the door, so that he'll step into it and fall when he comes in the room! Then we shall hear him."

"Yes. And we'll pile a whole heap of books nearby too, so that he'll knock those down and make an awful noise!" said Dan.

"And we'll wind string all about the place so that he'll get caught!" said Daisy.

"Then we really shall hear him and see him."

So they put out an empty box by the door, and built up an enormous pile of books nearby. Then Dan wound string here, there and everywhere! What a trap for poor Santa Claus!

The twins fell asleep. In the middle of the night they awoke with a jump. *Crash*! The pile of books had fallen over. Someone had trodden in the box and tripped into the books. And by the visitor's angry grunts it sounded as if he had been well caught by the string!

Neither of the twins dared to get out of bed and put on the light. They lay trembling in the darkness. Would Santa Claus be very cross with them?

Then they heard their father's voice, speaking in a low tone to their mother, who had come to see what had caused all the noise.

"These tiresome twins! They've put a box by the door and I trod in it and upset a pile of books or something and now I'm all caught up with string. I tell you, these children won't have a single thing in their stockings if this is the way they behave!"

Father and Mother went away. Dan and Daisy slipped out of bed, cleared up the mess, and took down the string. Then they hopped back to bed, glad that they had only caught Daddy, and not Santa Claus after all.

"Perhaps he will fill our stockings," whispered Daisy. He did – but they didn't deserve it, did they?

The Box of Magic

Once upon a time, when Muddle and Twink, the two brownies, were walking along over Bumblebee Common, they found a strange box lying on the path. Muddle picked it up and opened it.

"Twink!" he cried, in amazement. "Look! It's full of wishing-feathers!"

Twink looked and whistled in surprise. "Jumping buttons!" he said. "What a find! I say, Muddle, we'll have the time of our lives now, wishing all we want to! Come on – let's hurry home, shall we, and do a bit of wishing?"

Neither of the two naughty brownies thought that what they really ought to do was to find out who the box of wishing-feathers belonged to. No, they simply scurried to their cottage as fast as ever they could, Muddle carrying the box under his arm.

They ran in at their little front door, and put the box on the table. They took off the lid and there lay the wishing-feathers, dozens of them. Do you know what a wishing-feather is like? It is pink at the bottom, green in the middle, and bright shining silver at the tip – and it smells of cherry-pie, so you will always know one by that!

Well, there lay the pink, green and silver feathers, all smelling most deliciously of cherry-pie. Twink and Muddle gazed at them in delight. Twink picked up a feather.

"I wish for a fine hot treacle pudding!" he cried, waving his feather. It at once flew out of the window and in came a large dish with a steaming-hot treacle pudding on it. Unfortunately Muddle was in the way and it bumped into his head. The pudding fell off the dish and the hot treacle went down Muddle's neck. *Crash!* The dish broke on the floor.

"Ooh! Ah! Ooh!" wept Muddle.

"You silly creature!" cried Twink, in a rage, as he saw his beautiful pudding on the floor. "What do you want to get in the way for? Just like you, Muddle, always muddling everything!"

"You nasty, unkind thing!" said Muddle, fiercely. "Why didn't you tell me you were going to wish for a stupid pudding like this? Oooh! I wish the treacle was all down your neck instead of mine, that's what I wish!"

A wishing-feather flew from the box and out of the window as Muddle said this, and the treacle down his neck vanished – and appeared all round poor Twink's neck! How he yelled.

"I hate you!" he shouted to Muddle, trying to wipe away the treacle. "I wish you were a frog and had a duck after you!"

A wishing-feather flew out of the window once more – and, my goodness me, Muddle disappeared and in his place came a large green frog, who shouted angrily in Muddle's voice. Just behind him appeared a big white duck, saying "Quack, quack" in excitement as she saw the frog.

Then hoppity-hop went Muddle all round the room, trying to escape the duck. Twink laughed till the tears ran down his face and mixed with the treacle!

"Oh, you wicked rogue!" shouted froggy Muddle. "I wish you were a canary with a cat after you!"

Oh dear! Immediately poor Twink disappeared and in his place appeared a bright yellow canary, rather larger than an ordinary one. Just behind came a big tabby cat saying "Mew, mew!" excitedly at the sight of the canary. Then what a to-do there was! Muddle, still a frog, was trying to escape the duck, and Twink, a canary, was trying to fly away from the pouncing cat. Neither of the two had any breath for

wishes, and what would have happened to them goodness knows – if the cat hadn't suddenly seen the duck!

"Miaow!" it said and pounced after the waddling duck. With a quack of fright the white bird waddled out of the cottage, the cat after her. As soon as they went out of the door, they disappeared into smoke. It was most strange.

The frog and the canary looked at one another. They felt rather ashamed of themselves.

"I wish we were both our ordinary selves again," said Muddle, in rather a small voice. At once the frog and the canary disappeared and the two brownies stood looking at one another.

"This sort of thing won't do," said Twink. "We shall waste all the wishing-feathers if we do things like this, you know, Muddle."

"Well, let's wish for something sensible now," said Muddle. "What about wishing for a nice, big, friendly dog, Twink? We've always wanted a dog, you know. Now is our chance."

"All right," said Twink. "Let's wish for a black and white one, shall we?"

"No, I'd rather it was a brown and white one," said Muddle. "I like that kind best."

"Well, I prefer a black and white one," said Twink. "I wish for a black and white dog!"

Immediately a large black and white dog appeared, and wagged its tail at the brownies.

"I wish you to be brown and white!" said Muddle at once, scowling at his friend. The dog obligingly changed its colour from black to brown. Twink was furious. "I wish you to be black and white!" he yelled. The dog changed again, looking rather astonished.

"Now, don't let's be silly," said Muddle, trying to keep his temper. "I tell you, Twink, a dog is nicer if it is brown and white. I wish it to be . . ."

"Stop!" said Twink, fiercely. "It's my dog! I won't have you changing its colour like this! Wish for a dog of your own if you want to, but don't keep interfering with mine."

"I wish for a brown and white dog!" said Muddle at once. A large brown and white dog immediately walked in at the door, wagging its tail in a most friendly fashion. But as soon as the black and white one saw it, it began to growl very fiercely and showed its teeth.

"Grr!" it said.

"Grrr!" the other dog said back. The black and white dog then flew at the other and tried to bite it.

"Call off your horrid dog!" yelled Muddle to Twink. "It's biting mine! Oh! Oh! Look at it!"

"Well, you should have been content with one dog," said Twink. "You see, my dog thinks this is its home, and it won't let a strange dog come in. Quite right, too. It's a good dog!"

"It isn't, it isn't!" cried Muddle. "Oh dear, oh dear, do call off your dog, Twink. Look, it's biting the tail of mine."

"Of course it is," said Twink. "I tell you, mine is a very good, fierce dog. Tell your dog to go away, then it won't get hurt."

"Why should I?" shouted Muddle, in a temper again. "My dog has as much right as yours to be here. Isn't this my home as much as yours? Then my dog can live here if I say so! Oh look, look, your dog has bitten my dog's collar in half!"

Muddle was in such a rage that he ran to Twink's dog, his hand raised as if to smack it. The dog at once turned round, growled and tried to bite Muddle, who jumped away and ran round the room. The dog, thinking it was a game, ran after him, and Muddle was very much frightened.

"Call him off, call him off!" he yelled. But Twink sat down on the sofa and laughed till the tears ran down his long nose. He thought it was a funny sight to see Muddle being chased by his dog.

"I wish my dog would go and bite you, you horrid thing!" yelled Muddle. Then it was Twink's turn to jump up and run – for the brown and white dog ran at Twink, showing all its white teeth.

Twink ran out of the cottage followed by a snapping dog, and Muddle ran out too, the other dog trying to nip his leg.

"Oh!" cried Twink, as he was bitten on the hand.

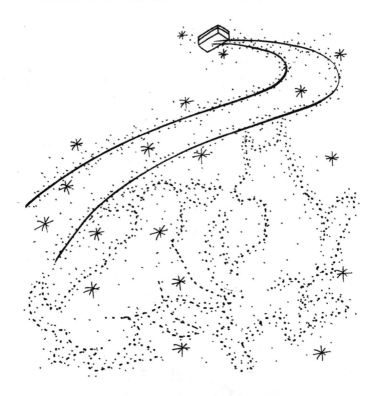

"Oooh!" yelled Muddle, as he was nipped in the leg. "I wish the dogs weren't here any more! I wish we hadn't got those horrid wishing-feathers that seem to make things go all wrong!"

In a trice the two dogs vanished and the box of feathers sailed away through the air, back to the Green Wizard who had lost them that morning. The two brownies stood looking at one another, Twink holding his hand and Muddle holding his leg.

"The dogs have gone but they've left their bites behind them," groaned Muddle. "Why didn't you wish those away too, Twink? The feathers have gone now, so we can't do any more wishing."

"Well, our wishing didn't do us any good, did it?" said Twink. "Come on in, Muddle, and let us bathe our bites. We have behaved badly and we deserve our punishment. My goodness, if I find wishing-feathers again, I'll be more sensible. Won't you?"

"Rather!" said Muddle, limping indoors. But I don't expect they ever will find such a thing again do you?